PALMETTO
P U B L I S H I N G
Charleston, SC
www.PalmettoPublishing.com

Paperback ISBN: 979-8-8229-3599-0
eBook ISBN: 979-8-8229-3600-3

JEFFREY HARRIS

To you, The Most High God,
all glory is yours.

To Kim and Jeff Harris,
Thank you.

PROLOGUE

It's funny how stories of heroes who died in war were exaggerated; it was always they died with courage, glory, and valor, but did they really? The only way to tell was by the look on their faces when they died. When their throat was cut, were they smiling? When an arrow pierced their heart, did they look proud?

The ground was layered with dead men. None were smiling or were proud. These were men who died scared, foolish, and regretful. The skies were soaked in blood as the myriad of aircraft battled, and smoke from bombs and bullets suffocated the air. Buddha Bane laid about, paralyzed. He bled out from the multiple bullet wounds that penetrated his armor. He could do nothing but die slowly and watch as his men were cut down with unprecedented weapons. This was their last stand; the enemy had made their way to his homeland. All his tactics, all his bravery, all his acute warriors were not enough to hold them back. The enemy held lightning in their hands, engaging from long distances and short. Their aircraft rained fire with so much ferocity that it even shook the ground and dismembered men. They faced an army, a force that none in this realm had ever witnessed.

Buddha saw his brother ten feet from him. He, too, suffered many bullet wounds, but he took one bullet to his head, making his death a swift one.

"Buddha!" She ran to his side. She was gorgeous, though words could do nothing to describe her beauty. She wore a transparent garment, revealing her dark skin, her black nipples piercing through. She adorned herself with gold chains, earrings, and bracelets, and strange tattoos covered her whole body. Her eyes were as blue as the ocean waters. Her black hair was braided in a unique style with golden ornaments. She held Buddha in her arms and wiped his bloodied hair out of his face.

"I'm—I'm sorry." Buddha coughed blood.

"Sorry for what? You fought with so much bravery. Only you... only you were brave enough to look evil in the eye and not falter," she said with watery eyes.

The enemy charged the grounds, shooting their weapons and commanding their soldiers, ignoring Buddha and the woman holding him.

"I can save you, but you have to make the deal, Buddha," she said. "Please make the deal."

Buddha was in so much pain. He grew cold, feeling his soul leaving his body. He looked at the woman, her face beautiful yet filled with worry. She had warned him years ago that an enemy would breach and devour the realm. Buddha Bane took the warning to heart, but after years of consistently winning many battles, he believed he had already defeated the enemy. He was wrong in his complacency.

"You can still win, Buddha. There is still time," she said.

"The next life." Buddha forced his words out.

The woman shook her head as tears ran down her face. "If they prevail, then I will be no more. I will forever be gone from you." She took his hand and grasped it. "Make the deal."

Buddha lifted his arm and pointed to his dead brother. "Him too."

The woman nodded. "If that is what you wish."

The sound was agonizing as the aircraft roared above them.

The woman looked away into the distance and then back at Buddha. "You don't have much time."

Another aircraft came soaring through the sky. Like a bird releasing its prey, it dropped a metal contraption that hit the ground, causing a fire that reached the heavens. The ground shook violently under

Buddha. He reached out to touch the woman's face, who delighted in the affection.

"Your name?" Buddha asked.

"Make the deal," she said.

Buddha nodded.

"Through the fire you will be reborn, Buddha," the woman said.

She continued to hold Buddha, unable to let him go as the fire encroached quickly and violently, turning everything it touched into instant ash.

———•—•——

Augustus Graves sat at the table of the Members Only Club, which maintained its handful of High-Top's wealthiest. Augustus made plenty of deals at the club. He delighted in the rule that no one was allowed to eavesdrop on another's conversation, and the level of confidentiality of what went on in the club was appreciated. But today he was not here to make business deals or gossip; a simple steak meal and quiet was all that he wished for. He coughed vehemently into his handkerchief, blood spotting on the cloth. He was older, as old as he'd ever been, and he despised it. He poured himself a strong alcoholic beverage and sipped it. He looked up to see a middle-aged man standing at his table.

"May I sit?" the man asked. He was at least six feet, his pale skin tan and perfect, not a wrinkle or blemish. His mane was a thick black, in a comb-over fashion. He kept his face clean-shaven and had a smile that could cripple you. He dressed as one would expect of an affluent man, dapper in his well-tailored plaid suit and black pointy dress shoes. He didn't wait for Augustus to give him permission; he sat down, crossed his legs, and lit a cigar.

"Wow, Augustus, you look like shit. How much longer do you have?" the man asked. The man was not wrong—Augustus did look like shit. He was once handsome with good hair and as strong as an ox. His black skin was now wrinkled and beaten, what was left of his hair now gray, and he was permanently hunched over. Yet his mind was still intact, and that was all he needed.

"What do you want?" Augustus asked, his voice low and cold.

"I wanted to see you one last time, you know, pay my respects. I'd rather do that while you're alive and can actually hear me." The man puffed on his cigar, relishing its taste. "Honestly, you had one hell of a fucking run, and you will be the first person in a long time that I will miss when they are gone."

"Did anyone ever tell you to never celebrate until victory is written?" Augustus asked rhetorically.

"Come on, what more can you do? The moment you're in the ground, your daughter takes the helm. Now she is a nasty bitch, but she ain't you. And well, your son, I mean, he is only one man. We are many."

Augustus poured himself another drink, ignoring the man.

"I mean, listen, you were a great adversary. I have been doing this for a very long time, and no one gave me such a headache such as yourself."

"Did you come here to gloat or suck my dick?"

The man smirked. "See? That's the shit I'm going to miss. Nobody has the balls to talk to me like that, and I'm going to fucking miss it. But anyways, I'm willing to let bygones be bygones."

"Oh yeah?" Augustus said with little care in the world.

"I want to extend a lifeline. Let me save you. Join us. Mortality is wasted on you."

Augustus laughed hard. He coughed, spitting blood into his handkerchief, and looked at the man who didn't get the joke. Augustus laughed again.

"The best part was that you were actually serious." Augustus wiped the tears from his eyes and gathered himself. "You still fear, don't you? Yeah, you still fear, and you have every right to. Shit, your best bet would be to put a bullet in my head right now."

"We are old men, Augustus. Fighting like that is beneath us." The man stood up to take his leave. "I meant it. I am going to miss you, but the breach will happen, and then the game is basically over. You fought a good fight. You have my respect. Goodbye, Graves."

My only regret in this life is missing out on the opportunity to kill you myself, Augustus thought as he watched the man go.

Scan QR Code to listen.
Echo
by
M.U.R.K Entertainment

PART ONE

1

Miles approached a building that appeared to be nothing but a hole-in-the-wall, hidden between two buildings. It had no name, which gave it a sense of conspicuousness. Its appearance explained why it lacked an influx of business during the day. Miles entered the restaurant and was surprised by how extraordinary it was inside. The floors were wooden, and both sides of the aisle were lined with black tables and benches. The lights were dim, and the purple curtains proved formidable against any outside light, giving the restaurant a pessimistic vibe.

I've been here for about a year now, and I've never been in this place.

He made his way to the bar, and the bartender directed him to the back of the restaurant. A large man dressed in an all-black designer suit guarded the back door. He sported dreadlocks and had an intimidating build. Miles took notice of the firearm slung around the guard's neck and held firmly in his hands.

"I'm here for Styles," Miles said.

The guard allowed Miles to walk through the door. The room was dark with dim lights and had no windows; it's the perfect meeting spot for someone who didn't want to be seen or heard.

Styles sat at one of the black tables, eating some kind of meat and vegetables. He was a slender, dark-skinned gentleman who wore glasses, and his salt-and-pepper beard was always lined to perfection. Miles couldn't remember the time when Styles had hair, but his bald head suited him well. Like his bodyguard, Styles wore a designer suit, but his suit's was more pleasing to the eye. The navy-blue suit with the white shirt and matching bowtie shouted respect.

"Come sit so we can get on with it," Styles said, gesturing to the seat in front of him.

Miles sat down, crossed his legs, and looked up at the second guard who stood adjacent to Styles, holding the same firearm as the first.

"Why do you always look like death follows you?" Styles asked, continuing to chew his food.

Styles commented in reference to Miles's appearance. Miles wore a long, stylish black coat, which hid the black shirt underneath. He sported black jeans and black boots. His hair was in two black braids down to his shoulders, and his sideburns were clean-shaven. The stubble in his beard showed gray hair trying to introduce itself on his brown skin.

"Why am I here, Styles?" Miles asked.

"I have good news," Styles replied, finally putting down his fork and sliding his plate away.

"Am I retiring?" asked Miles.

Styles, a man who had labored in law school, always used his best professional stance when delivering an answer, he knew someone didn't want to hear. He did so now.

"Retiring as of right now would not be in your best interest or your family's," Styles replied.

Spreading his hand apart in confusion, Miles asked, "Then why the fuck am I here? What the fuck was so damn urgent that you couldn't tell me over the damn phone?"

Styles coughed, smiled, and reached into a bag next to him to get his portable digital processor. He turned on the holographic mode, pulled out a manila folder, and opened it.

"The fuck is this?" Miles asked.

"Your last job."

Miles looked at him, confused. "You just told me I'm not retiring."

"That's because it has been decided that if you accomplish this last job, you'll be paid well. After which, we'll provide you with a new identity. You can live wherever you want if that is what you wish."

Miles stared at him blankly, and Styles continued.

"However, because you are the son of Augustus Graves, his blood always will run in your veins. But you will not be rewarded any shares or equity in the company in the event of any liquidation. You will not inherit any trusts or properties upon the death of your father, for obvious reasons. If you are to have any children, they will not be recognized in any way, shape, or manner. If there is anything else you will need, your sister will provide for you when she takes charge."

The room was silent for mere moments as Miles took it all in. He was never known for temper tantrums or showing anger even when he was angry, but today was different. Miles stared at Styles, who felt Miles's deep, cold brown eyes peering into his soul.

"I was looking forward to being done with all this shit, and you come here offering me a final job and a fucking severance package, basically saying if I'm done doing the bloody work, my family is done with me." Miles gripped both sides of the table to hold his anger. "I ought to fucking kill you, Styles."

The bodyguard adjacent to Styles made a motion to move.

"Whatever he is paying you, it ain't worth dying over." Miles warned the guard without taking his eyes off Styles. "But if you take one step toward me, I can't save you."

Unfortunately pride and ego were a bitch, and the guard started to take a step. He regretted it immediately when his knee buckled, bringing him down to his other. He choked on his own blood as he held his throat in a futile attempt to keep the blood in. Blood squirted everywhere, even on Styles, who was mortified. The bodyguard at the door rushed in after hearing the thud of the body hitting the floor. Without leaving his chair, Miles produced a hidden handgun and shot the guard in the head.

Rikii relaxed her Flex and stepped over the dead man soaking in his own blood. She closed her switchblade and walked to Miles with the grace of a model, sporting a pixie haircut with finger waves, a biker outfit, and combat boots. Her face was soft, with hazel eyes and tan skin.

"Hey, Styles," Rikii greeted as she rubbed Miles's shoulders.

Death always follows me, Miles thought.

"Rikii," Styles greeted, with nothing but pure irritation in his voice.

Styles looked at the blood spots on his suit, no longer in the mood to be professional.

"Yo, what the fuck is wrong with y'all?" he yelled.

"There's my cousin," Miles said, acknowledging the change in Styles's behavior.

"Leave that prissy lawyer bullshit for them boys back home."

"OK, you motherfucker. Fuck you and your boyfriend there."

Miles looked up at Rikii. "Well, that was rude." He kissed Rikii's hands, then stood up to leave. "I'm not doing the fucking job. Tell Daddy that for me."

"I'm trying to fucking help you, Miles!"

"How? I did everything that was asked of me, and this is the shit I get!"

"You wanted out, this is your fucking out! What the fuck did you expect, Miles? You have more bodies and blood on your hands than the hairs around your dick. And what, you thought you were just gonna go back home and take charge of the fucking foundation? Do you even know what an invoice is, Miles? Do you read and look over emails? You're a weapon, Miles, which is all you ever will be, so take the fucking deal!"

Miles was silent.

"Be fucking thankful this is what they gave you, offering you a goddamn retirement plan." Styles spoke to himself yet loud enough for Miles to hear. "The Bloody Hands in charge of the Graves Foundation, now that would be something."

Miles sat back in the chair.

Thirty-two years of being a company man and trying to make his father happy had rendered Miles a tired individual. A few million coins to basically go lie down in a ditch and die somewhere without complaint was definitely a right hook he hadn't seen coming. His great-grandfather built the Graves Foundation, but the reason why it soared to the heavens and became a superpower was due to all the blood on Miles's hands.

Fuck, just letting sleeping dogs lie, Miles thought.

"Bring me the whole damn bottle," Miles told the bartender.

Miles left Styles with cleanup duty, while he and Rikii made their way to some godforsaken bar where people went to get drunk and place their bets on fights. Miles, slightly drunk, fingered his glass, waiting for his bottle.

"So what are we going to do?" Rikii asked.

Miles looked at Rikii with his deep concentrating eyes. Though Rikii was a beautiful woman, it didn't faze Miles. She was born into this world with male intentions. Miles continued to stare, but he wasn't looking at Rikii. He was looking through her, pondering distant memories, mistakes, and decisions. Memories before he fell from grace and how his life would have been if he had made different choices in his youth. His bottle arrived, breaking the trance, and Miles set the task of becoming drunker.

"I regret it all. I mean, what the fuck did I know? I was a fucking kid, but I should have stopped it," Miles said.

Rikii stayed silent and allowed Miles to drink and vent, basically just another day.

"A few million coins is a pretty price, but I never once did this for the coin. They're cutting ties with me, abandoning me, and forgetting about me as if I were never in the family. But family is supposed to look out for one another—or so I thought." He took a swig from his bottle. "Fucking sick fuck, I swear. Three decades of being in the trenches and I see life completely different now."

Rikii leaned out to touch his knee. "I will never forget you or abandon you."

Rikii had done this dance plenty of times before. Miles would get into his feelings, and Rikii would be there to assure him that she would never leave his side. Miles always smiled in appreciation, but he needed to hear it regularly, and not once did Rikii ever mind.

"And that's why you're my family, Rikii," Miles said. "You're all I have, and I don't take that lightly."

"I know, baby. How about we go home so I can take care of you? You need a bath."

Miles laughed. "You're always taking care of me."

"And what brings Bloody Hands to my place of business?" asked a man who sat down next to Miles.

Rikii stood, ready to educate the man on what happens when someone abruptly intrudes, especially without the proper mannerisms, but Miles held up his hand, signaling her to sit back down.

Miles swiveled in his chair, facing the crowd that watched two men pound their faces in. "Transport."

"Transport? Are you telling me the authorities rounded up all your boosters?" asked the man.

"Air transport," Miles said, his eyes still on the crowd.

"I'll need some time."

"You have two days. The coin is good."

Laughing, the man responded, "You're out of your fucking mind if you think I can secure you air transport in two days."

"Baby, who is this, and why the fuck do we need air transport?" Rikii asked, worried about the answer.

Miles turned to look at the man, who had slicked-back, stringy, silver hair and missing teeth. "I don't need to fly it. I need to be cargo and be flown out of this district."

Rikii grabbed Miles under his chin and turned his face to hers. "You keep me in the dark now? Is this how we do it? You're fucking mad at me? Like, what the fuck?"

"Miles, I have a manifest being made up, but the cargo is expected to go out next week to Kurtaz. It's a contract. I can't deviate from it," the man said, ignoring Rikii's tantrum.

"Look, what can you do for me in a short period of time?" Miles asked.

The man took a deep breath, exhaled, and said, "If you can get to the Southern Isles, I know a guy who can get you on a freight craft."

"Nah, I need air transport out from First Landing to land in New Area undetected, and I need two seats." Miles held up two fingers.

The man whistled. "You're asking a lot there, Miles. That's gonna cost you a kidney. I think I have a way, but you're going to have to pretend to be cargo workers. You'll have to pay for my expenses and my friend's expenses. My friend is gonna have to lay off a couple men to get you and your lady on. He's not a prick, so he is gonna wanna give those men fair wages for the work they would have done."

The crowd roared again as the next two contenders came into the middle of the floor and began hashing it out. Rikii grew irritated, which Miles knew would eventually result in someone leaking blood onto the floor.

"You make good coin here, don't ya? Entrance fees, the bets, the drugs you're selling in the bathrooms, yeah, you make good coin here," Miles pointed out.

"What are you getting at?" the man said quizzically.

"How many people here know who I am?"

"To be honest, probably just me."

"Well, I'm about to pay all your expenses and your buddies right now."

"Yeah?"

"Bet on me." Miles nodded to the fight in the middle of the room. "Your best fighter, your champion, or whatever, just bet on me."

Pondering the idea, the man looked at the crowd of drunken idiots. "Are you sure you can win?"

Miles gave him a look of confidence and responded, "The coin you'll earn will pay not only for my and Rikii's seats but also for your own manifest not going out to Kurtaz as planned."

"What's the play here?"

"You know better than that." Miles gave the man a grim look.

"Don't bust my balls, Bloody Hands. I'm just seeing if you're sober enough to fight. Anyhow, you have to put on a good show. These fools here don't just pay for the blood. They pay for the entertainment too." The man got off his stool and walked into the crowd.

"Oh, one more thing," The man said, turning back to Miles.

Miles looked at him with an eyebrow raised.

"I want to add in a favor for payment as well. It's nothing out of your way. There is this slimy fuck named Dimitri who not only is trying to take over my drug business but also had the gall to hook up with one of my women," the man informed.

"Yeah, yeah, I get it. It will get handled. Just send me the details," Miles responded.

Miles gained the attention of the bartender and gestured to his empty glass.

"Another and make it stronger."

"Everything I fucking do for your ass, and you treat me like a side-kick," Rikii blurted out.

"Love, everything is fine," Miles reassured.

"How is it fine? I don't know the fucking plan, Miles."

"Neither do I. I'm making this shit up as I go," Miles said, looking at Rikii. "We're going to New Area for the job, and we'll figure out the rest."

"And why are we doing that? There is too much with this job. It doesn't make fucking sense," Rikii stated.

"Yeah, I know. Maybe I should start reading those emails," Miles joked. Rikii gave him a look that showed she was not in the mood for joking.

The silver-haired, toothless man signaled Miles to come into the ring.

"How about some luck before I go?" Miles suggested.

Rikii kissed Miles on the corner of his mouth and whispered in his ear, "Hurry this shit up. I'm hungry."

Miles, six feet tall, stood from his stool, kissed Rikii on her forehead, and headed to the ring.

"All right, all right, you miserable pieces of shit! Who's ready for the main event?" The silver-haired man roared to the crowd from inside the fighting circle.

The crowd cheered and roared.

"Tonight, we have an individual who believes his balls are smarter than his brain, for he wants to take on Vain, the Mad Titan." The crowd made sounds of delight. "Oh, you fatherless bastards, tonight is gonna make your pricks hard and your pockets fat because this match is a death match!" He looked at Miles in the fighter's corner and gave him a wink that indicated, "We all gotta make a living."

"Bring out the Mad Titan!" he shouted.

Vain came out and stepped into the fighter's circle. He had yellow skin, a bald head, and slanted eyes. There was a strange green creature with horns tattooed along the front side of his torso. Miles sized him up; Vain had to be over 6 feet and at least 230 pounds of solid muscle. What made matters worse was that Miles gauged he was former military because of his cutoff shorts that revealed his left augmented leg.

"Fighters, ready!" the silver-haired man yelled.

Miles took off his long black coat. He nodded, and his opponent did likewise.

———— • ————

Miles spat the blood from his mouth as he lifted himself off the ground. He turned and faced Vain, who was more than confident in his abilities. Vain came at Miles, swinging a right hook, followed by a left hook. Miles ducked both and went on the offense.

He delivered punches to the sides of Vain, who easily defended against them. Vain grabbed Miles by his shirt and headbutted him, making Miles stagger backward. Vain threw another right hook at Miles's jaw, who recovered, ducked the right hook, and punched Vain in the jaw. Vain's moment of shock was all Miles needed to gain a little footing. He charged Vain and delivered more punches to his body. Three punches to his right side and two on his left, followed by a left cross to Vain's jaw.

Miles was breathing heavily now. Vain shook his head in respect to Miles's abilities and turned it up. Vain charged Miles again, throwing a feint and spinning around to deliver a blow with his augmented leg to Miles's abdomen. Miles went flying into the crowd, knocking down a couple of drunken spectators.

Miles felt the pain shoot through him as he struggled to his feet. His guard went up as he circled around in the fighter's circle. Vain switched his style, standing with his left leg at the back, indicating he would be using it for more strikes. He delivered a quick strike to Miles's right knee, bringing him down. It was easy access for a right cross to Miles's face, which Vain took advantage of. Miles lay there, gathering himself. He looked at the crowd who cheered Vain on, all of them happy idiots.

OK, enough entertainment. This shit is really starting to hurt now, Miles thought.

Miles stood up and faced Vain. "Do all you slant-eyed boys hit like a bitch or just you?"

Vain came at him, throwing jabs. Two right hits landed, but Miles ducked the left one, maneuvering himself behind Vain. Miles threw two punches toward his back, hitting a kidney, and Vain collapsed onto the floor in pain. Miles rolled Vain onto his back and delivered several punches to Vain's face, blood splattering everywhere. Miles had to give Vain respect, for the big man took the pain and tossed Miles off him with brute strength. Miles rolled and got back to his feet. Vain struggled to stand as Miles ran and leaped off his right foot, with his right fist cocked back. He timed it right and shot his fist forward as he was coming down, landing a heavy hit to Vain's right eye.

Miles kicked Vain in the groin, grabbed his head, and delivered a knee strike to his forehead. Vain, now weak, grabbed Miles, hoping to weigh him down. Miles stepped on Vain's right foot and kicked his right shin several times; Vain loosened his grip. Miles threw a right cross, but Vain ducked and got behind Miles, wrapped his arms around Miles's waist, and heaved him up. Vain maneuvered his body to control Miles in midair, bringing him hard to the ground. All the air left Miles's lungs, and pain shot through him.

Vain stood above Miles and stomped on his chest with his augmented leg. He lifted his leg once more, but Miles rolled away. Before Miles got to his feet, Vain was on his back, his muscular arm around Miles's throat.

Miles felt the tightening and knew the match was over. Vain stood while still choking Miles, and he roared. The animated crowd cheered on the Mad Titan, except the silver-haired man, who'd just lost a shit ton of coin. Miles, struggling for air, noticed the silver-headed man's face, which held a look of dissatisfaction.

Miles winked at him, smiling, showing bloodied teeth. He put his feet together and swung them up, using the momentum to flip Vain forward onto his back. Vain got up and spin-kicked with his augmented leg, and a faint red hue illuminated Miles's body—his Flex activated. Miles allowed the hit to land against his head, and pieces of metal flew everywhere. However, it didn't shock Vain. He threw a right hook, and once again, Miles let it land. Vain roared in pain as he clutched his broken right hand. He attempted to kick Miles again, but Miles caught the augmented leg along his side. Vain, hobbling on one foot, tried to free his leg, but it was to no avail. Miles smiled at Vain, taking pleasure in his bemusement of Miles's strength.

"Just so you know, hell is very real," Miles said.

He kicked Vain in his groin repeatedly, and the big man went down in agonizing pain. Miles, who still had Vain's augmented leg tucked to his side, punched through what was left of the leg, ripping it from Vain's knee cap.

Vain did his best not to reveal shock as he lay on the ground, nursing his groin, his broken hand, and his leg's disappearing act. The crowd went silent, and an eerie quietness fell over the club as Miles approached Vain with what was left of his leg.

"Where did you serve?" Miles asked.

"MP-Delta Platoon of the Districts Army," Vain answered through tired and painful breaths.

"Well, soldier," Miles said, saluting Vain, "on behalf of the Districts...," Miles commenced, beating Vain with the remainder of his augmented leg.

Don't take this personal, big guy. I just had a real shit day.

He beat Vain with his own leg until the bone from his skull was clear to everyone. Miles, covered in blood, threw the leg down and surveyed the quiet crowd. He looked at the silver-haired man, who was smiling because of his sudden change in fortune.

2

The night was young, and the constellations in the black sky were symmetrically perfect. Jean noticed as he pulled into the driveway of his suburban home. He didn't rush to get out of the transport because he had his routine. Without it, his wife would shun him. He put out his cigarette in an empty soda bottle and screwed its top on. He leaned over to his glove compartment and took out a miniature toiletry bag. He removed a small bottle of lotion and applied some to his hands, masking the smell of cigarette smoke with a fruity smell. Next, he sprayed a bit of expensive cologne, one spray to his neck and one spray to his tie. Lastly, he took out a miniature bottle of mouthwash and rinsed his mouth, spitting the mouthwash out of his car. He put his toiletry bag into the glove compartment neatly and sat still, taking everything in.

He opened his visor and took a good hard look at himself in its mirror. At first, he was not pleased with what he saw. His slanted eyes were now accompanied by bags, his twenty-seven-year-old hairline had started the race of receding, and his patchy five o'clock shadow didn't do him any justice. But after stewing over how handsome he'd once been, it became irrelevant to him when he realized the sacrifice of his good looks was worth what he gained in its place. A yearlong bidding war for one thousand acres of land in Rae, a jungle in the country of Kurtaz, ended.

Twelve months ago, Jean was nothing more than a simple assistant to Michael Goodchild, owner of Good Tech. Michael got it in his head that he could create another manufacturing base for cheaper labor and build a tech utopia in a low-class country. But the real truth was that he heard that it was a gold mine, and whoever could control those lands could control the world. Unfortunately, there were two dilemmas with that dream.

First, there were other competitors looking into the land, and second, the government in control of the property was not selling. At least five corporations had gone head-to-head with the government of Kurtaz and offered them the stars and moon to purchase it. Finally, the Kurtazian government gave leeway, but it came down to who they could benefit from more.

Jean had worked endlessly day in and day out to help Mr. Goodchild and the board secure victory. The busy work took a toll on Jean's marriage and his ability to be a good father. To make matters worse, three months into the bidding war, Mr. Goodchild had suffered a heart attack that left him hospitalized. But that was not enough to stop Mr. Goodchild, and Jean saw an opportunity to shine. So he'd promised his boss victory as long as he put Jean in charge while the boss recovered. He had probably been a little out of his mind from the heart attack because Mr. Goodchild had agreed.

Jean hired the best private investigators to dig up all the dirt on each of Goodchild's competitors. He granted pay raises and overtime to the company's accountants so that they could hide all corruption within Good Tech. That maneuver proved useful; they hid everything where even God couldn't find it. He went to local clubs and found the most beautiful women and hired them to accompany him on his trips to Kurtaz while he visited the neighboring ancient cities of Rae. He planned to seduce prominent men to support his claim by promising them rewards if they allowed Mr. Goodchild to secure the acres in Rae. He even made women available when he invited several government officials of Kurtaz to the district of Old Alexandria. Jean dumped coin into hotels, expensive parties, and dinners, anything to make them feel like kings.

The private investigators did better than he imagined. They uncovered corruption, sexual harassment cases, negligence, and unethical experiments performed by the other competitors. The most damaging bit of information they uncovered was a bust by the International Banking Network aka IBN. Jean and his investigating team found foul play within their finances, which later proved the company and the companies involved with IBN were connected to the fall of Euphoria, an island caught in the crossfire of the Water Wars.

IBN public disgrace was enough to convince the government that Kurtaz would not be lucrative if associated with corporations who condone such behavior. In the end, Good Tech was offered the acres of lands for an astronomical price, but to Goodchild the cost meant nothing, for no one understood how far his coin stretched and would reach once he planted his flag in those lands.

Jean smiled at himself in the mirror. He couldn't wait to tell his wife that it was done and that all had not been in vain. Goodchild had offered him a raise and a bonus that would make even a rich man's jaw drop. Jean closed his visor and leaned over into the passenger seat to grab the bouquet of roses he'd bought to surprise his wife. He exited the car and walked to his front door with a new swagger. He entered his house and looked for his wife.

"Lauren!" Jean yelled with joy. "Where are you, baby?"

It felt good to be able to yell, which he could only do because his son was away at camp. Jean entered his dark house, stopping to place his keys on the stand next to the door. He figured his wife was sleeping, a luxury he now would never take for granted again. Jean walked into the kitchen, turned the lights on, and placed the roses in a vase for Lauren in the morning. He walked back down the hallway, to the front door, and to the stairway. He took off his coat and placed it on the banister of the bottom step, a bad habit of his. The staircase was pitch-dark, and so was the hallway.

"Baby?" Jean called after his wife as he walked up the staircase.

He walked and felt his way to the door of their master bedroom, which was closed. Jean thought it was odd; Lauren only liked the door closed when they were having sex. A strange scent filled Jean's nostrils. He cursed, deciding it was probably another dead rat in the vents. As quietly as he could, he opened the bedroom door. He peeked his head in, but his wife was not in the bed. Light shining from under a door across the room told him Lauren was in the bathroom.

Damn, it fucking stinks in here.

"Baby? I'm home. Are you okay in there? I smelled you all the way down the hallway," Jean said, smiling. There was no response, and Jean knocked again. "Lauren, I'm coming in."

Jean opened the door, and to his horror, blood was splattered on the bathroom walls, mirror, floor, sink, toilet—everywhere. He stepped back and vomited on his bedroom floor. He didn't want to go back in, but he had to. He had to face it. He had to answer the question that sprang into his head.

Jean mustered the courage to look into the bathtub.

His legs were weak, each step harder than the last.

With tears running down his face, he reached his arm out and drew back the curtain soaked in blood.

He fell to his knees in horror and pain as he found his wife dismembered. With dry heaves, he cried out in pain

Looking into his wife's eyes, he caressed her cheek and rubbed her blond hair now covered in blood. Something in her mouth caught Jean's attention. He was horrified to pick up his wife's head, but it was the only way to find out what it was. With blood-soaked hands, Jean opened his wife's mouth to find a folded piece of paper.

What the fuck is this madness?

He unfolded it, discovering it wasn't a piece of paper but a photograph. Jean rinsed it off in the sink, as it was soaked in blood. He held it to the light to reveal the photo of his son eating cake on his seventh birthday.

———·—·———

The Old Man woke from his nightmare, drenched in sweat. It'd been the same nightmare for twenty-two years. He dreamed of nothing else ever. His insomnia made him a perfect candidate for understanding how the nightlife operated in New Area. In the beginning, he ran numbers for a kingpin. However, it wasn't long before he'd made his move and dethroned the king. He ruled his territory with precise calculations and maliciousness.

He took control of the gambling business—anything with casinos, bets on fights, horses. You name it, it belonged to him. He even created security services for high-end celebrities who came into town. For years, his business was booming, then the Ryse came. The Old Man knew better not to fuck with one of the oldest secret societies in the Districts, let alone the world. They came into New Area, broke up territories, and established Barons. The Old Man kept his position and was given the title of baron, for which he paid a quarterly fee to the Ryse.

The Old Man looked into the mirror; he observed his body that told a story that he was a man of discipline who hid it underneath a myriad of tattoos. From his neck down to his legs, he was covered in ink. When he had realized that regardless of where he got a tattoo on his body, he couldn't feel a thing; he had become addicted to them. His head was mainly bald, his eyebrows faded but contained strings of black and white hair. He kept his face clean-shaven.

The Old Man got dressed. He wore his standard black suit, white top, and red tie, along with driving gloves, which covered his bruised and scarred hands. He walked through his penthouse suite, decorated with expensive wall art that spoke of ancient tales of wars, gods, and proverbs. He made sure to look at each piece of art before he left, granting silent goodbyes and giving thanks to their wisdom. He stopped to appreciate the view from his suite. He could see the entirety of New Area, lit up in the night. He felt the view itself could be a wall piece. *Shit, why not?* It seemed as if he spent more hours looking out of that window than doing anything else.

"You ready, sir?" a young man, head full of combed black hair and dressed in a black suit, white top, and red tie, asked from the front door.

The Old Man nodded and looked back at his penthouse one more time. Times were changing. A new threat came to New Area, and it turned things upside down. The consequence of which was that the barons and the Old Man had to answer for it. He smiled and walked toward the front door.

"Young man," he said, "good things come to those who wait."

"You're in high spirits today, sir. What's the occasion?" the young man asked.

Vengeance.

3

Sandy beaches and fruity drinks, Miles thought as he extracted the teeth from the squirming man handcuffed to the metal chair.

The man yelled in pain, begged for mercy, and screamed from the top of his lungs for help. They were in an abandoned warehouse with no soul in sight. Miles ignored the pleas. He moved with finesse, yanking out tooth after tooth.

"Oh, these houses are gorgeous," Rikii said as she sat atop an old desk, looking at houses for sale on her portable digital processor, or PDP. Rikii wore a white T-shirt, tight ripped black jeans, and laced-up heels with snake print—her style flawless.

"Should we get a pool?" she asked.

The man yelled in pain as Miles extracted another tooth from his mouth.

"The pool is a must. Think about the parties, Rikii," Miles said.

Rikii shrugged and continued her house search. Pool or not, Rikii was just glad Miles was OK with her following him into his new chapter in life. Ever since their first job together eight years ago, Rikii had not left Miles's side. She couldn't imagine herself living a life without him.

"Please, please," a woman's voice said.

Miles turned his attention from the man and looked at the woman sitting in the corner, handcuffed to a rusted pipe. Her salt-and-pepper hair was disheveled. Her pale skin was even more pale from fright, which didn't go well with her running makeup.

"Why are you doing this to us? We are good people," she begged for answers.

Miles looked at the man, who was drooling blood, his dark skin wrinkled from age, then looked back at Rikii with dissatisfaction.

"I am so sorry. We are over here talking about pools and shit. I didn't even realize I haven't shown you good hospitality. Are you thirsty? Hungry, perhaps?" Miles asked. "Rikii, can grab you some chips or something?"

The woman was dumbfounded. Her husband's teeth were being pulled from his mouth by a strange man with no explanation, and this man thought her stomach was of any concern.

"Hey, baby, you might want to check this out." Rikii hopped off the desk and showed Miles her PDP. She fiddled with it for a second and put it in hologram mode, which lit the dull room.

The news anchor was a pale-skinned woman with brown hair, nice eyes, and a skinny build. She was wearing a yellow business suit top. "We have breaking news." Her voice was professional but anxious.

"At approximately 1700 hours, Rasheeda, the capital city of Kurtaz, has fallen to the Invaders."

The anchor paused for a minute as pictures and a video footage of the capital's building appeared behind her. The video showed buildings being blown up and men wearing all-black tactical gear, celebrating throughout the streets by shooting their firearms into the sky.

"No one can predict the future, but the five-year war in Kurtaz seems to be coming to a close. We have knowledge that what's left of their government is in talks of a surrender."

Miles touched the screen of the PDP, minimizing its hologram feature. "It seems like we are running out of time,

"Baby, we stick to the plan. We are almost there." Rikii walked over to Miles, who sat rubbing his arm, deep in thought. "Remember, sandy beaches and fruity drinks." Miles smiled at her, thankful for being his backbone. "Can I ask you something?"

Miles didn't turn or look up from pulling out his hostage's teeth. "Of course."

"Do you or have you thought about wanting kids?" Rikii said, with a tone that showed she wasn't too sure of the question herself.

This time Miles turned to her. "Do I look like I would be good father material? Come on, now you know my pops. Us Graves should not procreate."

"I don't think that at all about you. I believe you would make a great dad."

"Yeah, I guess I will do what my daddy did to me, huh? Have the kid train to kill day in, day out like it's the fucking end of the world or something." Miles looked at his hostage and decided that he had enough. He undid his handcuffs and, lifted the older man out of the seat, and dropped him to the floor. He made his way to the woman, who screamed and begged for her life.

Rikii walked over and slapped her hard enough to quiet her screaming. Rikii released her from her restraints, and Miles heaved the woman up.

"Please, please, I have coin. I will give it all to you," the woman said as she was escorted to the chair that her husband was previously sitting in, her pleas ignored.

Miles strapped her to the metal chair, and with his pliers, he went to extract her teeth.

"Open your mouth," Miles ordered the woman, who held her mouth shut.

Rikii stood over the woman's husband, who lay unconscious on the floor, bleeding from his mouth. She drew her firearm and pointed it at his head.

"Open your fucking mouth for him, or I will blow your husband's brains out of his head."

The woman obliged, fear transparent on her face.

"What's with all this kid shit anyway? You want a kid?" Miles asked.

Rikii walked back to her desk and sat upon it. "I don't know. Maybe. Do you think..." Rikii gathered her thoughts. "You think I would be a good parent?"

Miles yanked a tooth from the woman; she spasmed, and tears ran down her face along with blood.

"Rikii, you would be good at anything you want to do," Miles said, hoping it was enough comfort.

———•———

Miles threw the woman into the trunk of an old, rusted transport. She lay defeated next to her husband, with blood-soaked rags in both their mouths. Rikii took out her PDP, pointed it at the aged couple, and signaled Miles. Miles took his firearm from his lower back and shot both of them in the head. Rikii looked at Miles, whose all-black tank shirt was wet with blood and sweat.

"All right, I got it all saved," Rikii said.

Miles looked to the blue sky and observed the birds freely flying.

Soon I will be free too. So close.

"Are you ready for the party tonight?" Miles asked.

"Damn right. I already got my outfit picked out." Rikii shook her hips and stuck out her tongue.

Miles smiled at Rikii and motioned her to grab the red container from the back seat of the transport. Rikii drenched the transport and bodies with gasoline while Miles lit a cigar. He took a few puffs and flicked it into the trunk, watching the transport burst into flames.

Sandy beaches, fruity drinks.

Miles stared at Rikii. The feeling of his eyes on her made her look at him, and their eyes locked. Rikii knew Miles all too well. She knew when he was hungry, tired, or angry. She knew his cues when she needed him to strike a target; she knew him. Most importantly she knew when he couldn't hold back his urges for her, and it pleased her.

Rikii's smile faded, smelling the lust coming from Miles, her own desires radiating. She made her way closer to him, his eyes micromanaging her every step.

She stopped within arm's reach of him, and like two magnets, a centimeter apart, the attraction became inevitable.

Miles gave in first, quickly grabbing Rikii by her neck, and kissed her. His tongue delighting in her taste, he held her by the waist, digging deeper into his lust. Rikii broke from his grasp and slapped him.

Miles looked at her as she walked past him back to the warehouse. She stopped, looked back, licked her lips, and gave Miles a wink, then continued to walk to the warehouse.

The flames of the transport grew and burned as hot as Miles's love for Rikii. Watching her walk, Miles was in a trance as he obsessed over Rikii's legs and backside as she strutted away. He stalked her all the way back into the warehouse, his urges impatient.

The sound of Rikii's heels echoed as Miles entered the warehouse. She leaned against the desk she sat on earlier, waiting for him; Miles wasted no time.

He rushed to her, lifting and placing her on the desk.

He kissed her neck, absorbed her aroma, and nibbled on the sensitive parts of her neck, listening to her slight moans.

He kissed on her lips passionately, then pushed her down onto the desk.

He undid her pants and yanked them off along with her undergarment. Rikii's heels made it hard to get her pants off—they settled at her ankles.

Rikii was raging, her privates erect and ready.

Miles took her into his mouth and Rikii gave a loud moan. She curled her toes toward her heels and grabbed ahold of Miles, giving him the look of ecstasy. The sound of him slurping drove her to satisfying pleasures.

"Keep going, baby," Rikii said.

Miles continued his passion, and with the saliva that was on her, he used it to lubricate the crevice of her butt.

"Oh fuccckk," Rikii moaned, feeling Miles's finger brushing over her hole.

Miles stood up and pulled Rikii to the end of the table and placed her legs on his left shoulder.

Miles spat into his hand, lubricated his own manhood, and slowly inserted himself into Rikii.

Miles grunted in pleasure, while Rikii, mouth open, rolled her eyes back. He took it slow at first, but his hunger was not in the mood for lovemaking.

Miles put his hand around Rikii's throat as he thrusted harder and faster; sweat pouring from his face. With nothing to grip, Rikii held on to Miles's arm that had her by the throat. She later pulled his hand from her throat and began sucking on his fingers. She whined with every thrust.

Miles pulled out, took hold of Rikii, and placed her on the floor, making her get on all fours. He grabbed his coat and handed it to Rikii, who automatically knew to take it and place it on the floor. He pushed her down, making her arch back her face in his coat.

"You love me?" Rikii asked.

"I belong to you," Miles said as he inserted himself back into her.

The feeling was unbelievable to Miles. He had his fair share of sexual partners, but none of them ever gave him the keys to their soul.

Miles thrusted, and Rikii's noises made him want to give her the world and beyond. Nothing else mattered to him, only Rikii. Miles always made sure the world revolved around her. He couldn't describe in words his love for her. He was always yearning for her in some fashion. He adored her. He never yelled at her even when they disagreed on topics. His patience with her was unprecedented. She could do no wrong in his eyes. He knew no matter her decision, he would never judge her. She would have his full support, no questions ever asked. The only thing he would consider a sin was her no longer loving him.

Miles grunted as he thrusted, unable to take his eyes off Rikii.

Rikii knew. She knew the love Miles had for her, and she felt his love every second of the day. When he would look at her in adoration, even when covered in blood from killing a target, that look would quickly lead into animalistic sex. Rikii loved Miles's kisses, for they were something different, Miles always kissed like he was savoring every moment of it. And when they would make passionate love, she would have to wipe the tears from his eyes because he struggled to find words to express himself. She would help him save face and blame it on sweat. Her soul, mind, and body were his, like his was hers. She would always be available to him, for he would be likewise.

Rikii looked back at Miles. "You finish when you're ready?"

The mere whisper of her voice was all he needed to complete his desire. With a massive grunt followed with a loud roar, Miles emptied himself inside her.

Miles, exhausted, fell to the floor, his chest heaving. Rikii lay on the floor next to Miles, smiling at him and caressing his face.

"You good, love?" Rikii asked.

Miles, still catching his breath, nodded and laughed to himself on how ridiculous he must look.

"It's too bad you couldn't hold it," Rikii said.

"And why's that?"

"Because when you see my outfit tonight, you're gonna wish you held it."

Miles slid himself closer to Rikii. "Now you know I'm full of surprises."

"Mm-hmm," Rikii responded as she and Miles began passionately kissing.

———— · ————

The music was booming, and the crowd soared. Men of all social status watched women glide up and down poles. The women were drop-dead gorgeous. Except for the stripper boots they wore, they were fully naked. They were collecting coins left and right. Men were sending coins their way as if they were in no need of it themselves. When a stripper was collecting coins, their names and the amount they earned showed in a holographic image above their heads from a mini device located behind their ears.

The club was crowded, but it didn't faze Roman. His swag shouted respect, and people would move or say "Excuse me" when he walked through. Miraculously he discovered a free couch and table and decided to lay claim to it.

A fully naked young lady approached him with a tray full of drinks.

"Can I get you something, honey?" she asked.

Roman examined her through his sunglasses. She was light-skinned and wore her hair in a ponytail. She wore a face full of makeup, and her breasts were full, her nipples dark and hard. Roman reached into his pocket and pulled out a hard business card. It was all black with no words or numbers on it.

"Take this to whoever is in charge now," Roman ordered.

The young lady was turned off by his tone, but because of how Roman was dressed and carried himself, she did as she was told assuming he was someone highly influential. She believed it even more when she touched the card, and the name Ryse appeared in gold lighting.

Roman examined the club and bobbed his head to the music. Within ten minutes, the same young lady returned.

"Follow me, honey," she said and led the way through the club. "Where you from?" She tried to get a sense of who he was.

Roman was dressed in all white, his trench coat decorated with gold buttons that covered a linen white tank top.

His pants matched his coat, held with a belt and gold designer emblem.

He wore no jewelry, but his sunglasses were round with a pink tint.

The young lady admired how handsome he was, his skin dark and smooth, his face serious, his hair black, and his beard full with strands of gray. They walked through the back of the club to a door that revealed a staircase.

"Up there, honey. Knock three times, and someone will let you in," she instructed. "After you're done maybe—"

Roman didn't wait till she finished her statement. He made his way up the staircase and knocked three times as instructed. The door opened, and a fat man in a cheap suit stood inside. Roman looked at him and the man gestured to the back of the room, where there were four people sitting around a small table. Roman went to the table, and someone brought him a chair.

"We're glad you could make it," a man said. He was pale-skinned and wore a slicked back hairstyle, a collared shirt, and slacks.

Roman looked at the three other people at the table. A woman, who appeared mature, was seated in a chair, wearing a copper satin dress that flattered her cleavage. Her dress complemented her caramel skin and jet-black hair. Beside her was an older man with yellow skin, slanted eyes, and a bald head. He was dressed in a traditional black suit with a white top, a red tie, and black driving gloves covering his hands. Beside him was a young man dressed in a trendy outfit that the youth followed. He wore blue jeans with a matching denim jacket covering a white shirt. His complexion was dark, and he had a hairstyle that reminded Roman of someone militant.

Roman removed his glasses, folded them, put them in his coat pocket, and crossed his legs.

"My employer is not happy," he said. "They appointed each of you as baron not because they wanted to but because each of you made an agreement that if my employer put you in a position of power, you would deliver."

He let his words sink in for a moment before he continued. He noticed he had their full attention, like a father speaking to his children.

"There is an agreement with each of you and my employer that you will pay a set price quarterly for your tenure as baron," he said. "But as of last year, none of you have been delivering the set price."

"You don't understand what we are dealing with here," the pale-skinned man nervously whispered.

"Enlighten me," Roman responded.

There was a slight pause, as the barons looked at one another, deciding who would speak.

The Old Man volunteered his services, and with a low, raspy voice said, "Bloody Hands."

The room was quiet, giving the name even more power.

"Are you telling me Bloody Hands is here in New Area and is methodically fucking over each one of you?" Roman asked.

"He fucking came out of nowhere and started strong-arming our businesses and hindering operations," the pale-skinned man informed Roman.

"How do any of you know it's Bloody Hands?" Roman inquired.

The three barons looked at the Old Man. Roman picked up on this and focused his attention on him.

"I'm waiting," Roman said, impatient with the Old Man, who seemed to zone out.

"In my youth, I have seen him, and once you see him, you never forget what he looks like," said the Old Man.

"Really?" Roman thought aloud.

"Listen, from the way you dress, I know for a fact that you don't live under a rock," the pale-skinned man said.

"You know, ever since I was a kid, the legend of Bloody Hands was like old folklore. But as I grew older, I heard the talks." The pale-skinned man pulled on his cigarette, sweating profusely. "You know what they say here? A car accident happens and a woman and her child die. They don't say it was an accident or bad luck, they say 'Bloody Hands.' A man down on his luck in life blows his own brains out. They don't say suicide, they say 'Bloody Hands.' People randomly go missing, series of murders, terrorist attacks. They don't say criminals, they say 'Bloody Hands.'" The pale-skinned man finished his cigarette. "I'm not built nor equipped with personnel to battle the motherfucker that retired the fucking devil."

Roman knew of Bloody Hands, but he never believed the hype; he was more than confident in his own abilities and the resources of his employer.

"You're not doing much talking," Roman said to the young man, who sat quietly and observed the conversation. "To be honest, I don't recognize you. You're not Jamal. Why are you here?"

The young man cleared his throat and said, "Jamal is dead. I took his place."

"Bloody Hands?" Roman asked.

The young man nodded.

Roman got comfortable in his seat. "How?"

The young man was confused by the question. "Sir?"

"How the fuck did Jamal die by Bloody Hands?"

The young man looked at the other barons who nodded at him to tell his story.

4

Jamal sat in the back of his well-decorated transport. It had white leather seats, blue neon lights in the door panels, built-in televisions on each of the back passenger windows, and an armrest that contained glasses of champagne. He sat and lit his cigar, puffing out smoke and basking in his glory. He was a two-time original gangster with a body count of nine, and he was proud of it. He sported an expensive navy blue sports jumpsuit with matching white sneakers, a gold chain around his neck, and a gold watch to complement it.

"We are almost at the port, Big J," his driver informed him.

Jamal ignored him, leaned back, and enjoyed his TV on the passenger window across from him. He'd earned the right to ignore motherfuckers beneath him. He had gone from being raised in the west end of New Area to hustling corners, robbing, killing, and even doing time in prison. By the time he was twenty-two, his crew, the Loud 20s, led in occupying most neighborhoods. By the time he was thirty-five, a group called the Ryse came in and started flipping the script on shit.

The shift in power didn't sit well with Jamal until he was granted the title of baron in his territory. He didn't understand at first, but later he was more educated on his new role; it was simple. Keep doing what he'd been doing and pay a quarterly fee to the Ryse. He would keep his seat and his life and be free to rule as he saw fit with minimum authority interruption. Five years later, he still sat on the throne.

"We're here," his driver said.

Jamal waited for his driver to walk around and open his door. He stepped out and examined his surroundings. It was early morning, and the morning fog was approaching. Three of Jamal's men stood on the port watching the port crane maneuver a green shipping container.

"Y'all made sure this was the right one?" Jamal asked.

"Yeah. We was hoping to have it on the ground before you got here, Big J, but the workers was on some other shit today," one of the men responded.

"Yeah, it's always something with this fucking port," Jamal said, puffing on his cigar as the port crane finally lowered the green shipping container.

The men approached the container, and Jamal watched as they lifted the latches above the handles, fully opening it. The container was filled with crates. Jamal's men opened a few crates and signaled to Jamal to come and observe. They were full of handheld firearms, shotguns, grenades, rapid fire rifles, and other weapons.

"OK, good shit. Get this moved," he ordered. Jamal's PDP rang. It was Lil P, his right-hand man.

"Yo, what's good?"

"Yo, we need you at HQ. We got a situation," Lil P said.

"What you mean?"

"We got a dude here saying he got a message for you. This motherfucker won't talk or say anything unless you here."

"OK, bet. Hold tight."

He signaled his driver. They returned to the transport and peeled out.

———————— • ————————

Back in the Day

"Stay strong, boys," Maximus ordered through his helmet that guarded his whole head, swinging his sword into his enemies. The white-uniformed teammates joined their leader in defeating the on-coming enemies. No one enjoyed battle more than Maximus—to him, it was similar to men paying coins to have their pricks played with. But Maximus would give a lot more to be in the presence of glory. The adrenaline of battle excited him, and the clashing of swords gave Maximus life.

Maximus deliberately positioned his team in the worst tactical po-sition. He wanted to enjoy the adrenaline rush. The game was simple; the last group standing won. It was one of the many training activi-ties that they performed in the jungles of Rae. There were five teams of four, all divided by their uniforms. Each trainee was armed with one handgun that contained one magazine of rubber ammo and one sword that illuminated blue on the sharp end. The blue fluorescent light on the blade was to prevent anyone from being cut and to send electronic messages of fatal blows, which would illuminate red on the trainees. Anyone who received less than a fatal blow would lose life points, and when all life points reached zero, you were disqualified.

"Don't let them grab the firearms, boys," Maximus ordered his team as he dug his blade in and out of his opponents.

There was a container full of firearms with rubber ammo, free for all teams. Maximus, apt in firearms, preferred blades. He and his white-uniformed team circled the container, taking out the fools des-perate enough to retrieve the firearms.

Maximus noticed a new team, their uniform green, coming straight toward him, their swords drawn. His first opponent was of average stature, screaming and swinging his sword one-handed at him. Maximus ducked two of his swings and delivered a deadly strike to his throat. His blade registered it was a fatal blow and sent a message to his opponent's wrist guard that he was out of the game. He turned and lowered his shoulder and scooped up the second opponent coming for him, flipping him to the ground. Maximus buried his sword into his abdomen; his opponents wrist guard acknowledging the fatal blow.

Maximus was greeted with a third opponent, who brought his sword down diagonally, aiming to cut the neck or chest, and once avoided, he brought his blade back up in an effort to try again. His speed was surprising, and Maximus was extremely quick to avoid the first strike, but his reaction time to the second strike was not sufficient.

The blow caught his armor and nicked the left side of his neck, nothing fatal. But Maximus lost life points, which was equivalent to losing blood.

Maximus assumed his opponent would then bring his blade down vertically, aiming for his head. His assumption was right. His opponent needed to bring his sword up in a circular motion to deliver the blow.

Maximus caught the wrist of his opponent's sword hand moments before the fatal blow landed, and he drove his sword into his opponent's stomach. He shoved his opponent to the ground, and the fourth enemy came quickly, taking advantage of Maximus's leaving his left side open for a strike.

Maximus put his left arm up, materializing a circular blue shield from his armguard that he wore from his wrist to the middle of his forearm, as the trainee began striking with basic maneuvers at him. He used his brute strength to knock back his opponent with his shield, creating space between them. The opponent charged him, bringing his sword down vertically. Maximus used his shield to block the blow but quickly went on the offense by using his sword to uppercut his opponent's torso.

All his opponent's life points were reduced to zero, a fatal blow. Maximus smiled at victory. He looked about the field, his fellow teammates fighting with valor. To put away firearms and use swords was the test of a true warrior's ability.

Maximus fiddled with his armguard, and a holographic screen had formed. He looked to see how many more trainees were left, and to his satisfaction, only his team and one from the black-uniformed team remained.

Too easy.

Maximus heard the sounds of his three teammates using vulgar language as their wrist guard gave off indication that they had received fatal blows.

"How the hell?" Maximus asked, puzzled.

His teammates couldn't tell him who it was. They didn't even see an enemy, and even if they did, that would defeat the purpose of them being dead.

An enemy we couldn't see. That could only mean someone is using their Flex. And only one person can use a Flex like that.

"Rikii!" Maximus shouted. The grounds were cleared from disqualified teams, which left only the container of firearms, Maximus, trees, and Rikii. "Bring your ass out here. Stop Flexing like the bitch you are, and let's do this shit!"

Maximus, only seventeen years of age, was one of the trainees who excelled in combat training, and he was one of the few who could use his Flex from a younger age, so he always had an advantage. But he knew Rikii could use her Flex as well, and it was just as dangerous.

Rikii, only sixteen, relaxed her Flex and faced Maximus, her uniform black.

"I don't get you. You've been doing weird shit ever since we were kids and found out your ass just wanted to be a girl the whole time. So explain to me why you didn't use your Flex to get rid of your dick and balls?" Maximus taunted.

"Well, I kinda need my dick if I want to fuck you in that pretty ass of yours," Rikii said.

Maximus grew irate; Rikii always made him uncomfortable. He never liked the way she looked at him and other boys while they had their daily showers. He didn't like the way she always tried to talk like the female trainees. When they were younger, he caught Rikii trying to stuff her shirt with tissues acting as if she had breasts. Maximus made a scene about it and made everyone laugh at and heckle her.

"Why don't you just give it up? I am better than you. I always have been, and I always will be. You're nothing but a short, scrawny little bitch," Maximus said as he prepared his fighting stance.

Rikii remained quiet and prepared her fighting stance and quickly activated her Flex.

Maximus wasted no time to charge; he activated his Flex.

He swung his sword in a swoop, attempting to deliver a fatal blow to Rikii's head.

Rikii was flexible. She ducked and moved backward to avoid the attack; her Flex masking her whereabouts.

Flex still activated, Maximus was fast, and as soon as he saw his attempt fail, he recovered himself and brought his sword from above his head. Maximus was apt in battle, and he knew he could see Rikii when he paid attention to the ground. Even though camouflaged, someone always made a mistake. And Rikii's flaw was that she wasn't light on her feet, and Maximus could read her footwork based on grass, leaves, and sticks being broken when she moved.

Rikii anticipated the move and rolled away to avoid it, yet Maximus Flexed, giving him abnormal speed, and he was on Rikii before she could fully recover.

The sword came downward, and Rikii used the flat side of her blade to block the attack. The force from the strike kept Rikii on her knees and knocked out her Flex; she couldn't manage to hold both her Flex and fight back Maximus's strength.

Maximus backed off, allowing Rikii to stand.

"I bet you like being on your knees, you fucking cunt," Maximus said.

Maximus relaxed his Flex for it was using too much of his stamina. He charged Rikii and swung a series of strikes, only to have them parried.

Rikii twirled her sword in her hands and swung it backhanded at Maximus, who ducked it and sliced at Rikii's leg, spilling life points. Maximus pressed on, and the clashing of weapons continued.

Maximus swung his blade, creating an opening to stab Rikii in her stomach. She sidestepped the blow and caught Maximus's arm under hers. Rikii was never one to put on muscle, but her strength came from anger, and it could not be denied. Maximus tried to free himself; he was rewarded with a headbutt from Rikii. Their helmets clashed, and both Maximus and Rikii lost life points.

 Maximus staggered backward, misjudging Rikii's combat skills. She delivered a front kick to his abdomen, sending him to the ground. Rolling to his feet, Maximus recovered himself and was greeted with vicious attacks.

Rikii landed a strike across the side of Maximus's helmet, and he fell hard, life points reduced significantly. Maximus thanked the gods that it wasn't fatal. He wouldn't be able to explain how he lost to Rikii, of all people.

Both fighters were tired, and the breathing became heavy between them. Rikii charged Maximus, twirling her sword, spun around, and swung her blade at Maximus's legs, scooping him off his feet. She instinctively kicked Maximus in his head, knocking his helmet off, showing his handsome features that were decorated with blood and dirt.

Maximus activated his Flex and moved quickly to the firearm container, taking out a rapid-fire weapon. He went to aim, but Rikii had already activated her Flex and couldn't be seen.

Maximus looked at the ground to see if he could read her patterns, but it was to no avail; he fired anyway. He unleashed a series of ammunition haphazardly, hoping one of the rounds would land and secure him victory.

Rikii, using her Flex, hid on the other side of the container, waiting for her moment. She remembered the harassment Maximus put her through growing up, how he made the other boys and girls isolate themselves from her.

Rikii remembered how they would steal the nail polish she bought with her allowance.

She remembered the night she was alone in the shower, and Maximus and his followers jumped her. They punched her. Some of them who had belts whipped her, while some stuffed their socks with bars of soap and hit her. She didn't want to be seen at all after that beating, and that's all she could think about until one day no one saw her at all.

Present Time

The transport crept up on the street, which was illuminated by the streetlights. The houses were old single-family homes that housed fallen sons and daughters of the Loud 20s. The rusty all-black transport was camouflaged perfectly under the night sky. Rikii turned off the headlights and left the car in neutral as she pulled up to the rundown, all-white two-story home that had Loud 20s members out in front, smoking, drinking, and doing a shit job at keeping guard.

"Yo, who pushing that whip over there?" someone asked as he pulled his handgun.

"Fuck, G, I don't know who that shit is, headlights off and shit," someone else responded.

"Yo, let me get a young blood to check that shit out," someone said.

A young man—no older than fifteen, wearing bandannas with Loud 20s colors of yellow and blue—walked up to the transport to investigate.

"Aye, ain't no one in this shit," the young man informed.

"What the fuck, you—"

A gunshot fired close to the man. He felt warm liquid that he realized was blood from his homie next to him. He went to aim his firearm in the direction of the shot, but he saw nothing, then everything went dark for him.

Rikii blew the heads off the two men, who seemed to be in charge. Everyone who saw what happened quickly dispersed into the street and into the backyards of neighboring houses. Rikii continued to use her Flex as she entered the house and shot everyone she saw.

Two men ducked under the couch, staring out the window, looking for the intruders. Rikii walked up to them and emptied her shotgun; they died ignorant of what happened.

There was someone in the kitchen who had the bright idea to just start shooting at air, but his aim was off, and Rikii shot him in the chest, sending him into the refrigerator.

"LJ, what's good down there?" someone yelled from the top of the staircase; he received no answer.

He held his handgun in both hands and walked slowly down the steps. He reached the bottom step, and Rikii, without faltering, shot him in the side of the head. His brain matter splattered over the walls and stairs.

Rikii walked up the stairs, kicked every door down, and cleared out each room until she reached the last room. Sounds of cartoons came from a TV. She kicked the door and saw a woman clutching her five-year-old son. Rikii relaxed her Flex, and the woman looked astonished at Rikii's beautiful features.

"Call him now," Rikii ordered the woman.

"Call who?" the woman asked.

Rikii answered by reloading her shotgun and pointing it at the boy.

"OK, OK, OK, I am calling him now," the woman said, suddenly eager to please.

"Put the call on holographic mode," Rikii ordered.

The woman did as she was instructed; the PDP rang and rang.

— · —

Way Back in the Day

"So Latoya is still mad at you?" Troy asked.

"What woman wouldn't be?" Augustus asked rhetorically. They stood behind the one-way mirror as they watched from holographic screens the surgeons beginning to make an incision on the head of Augustus's one-year-old son.

"The only way we're going to find out if our Nano-Secs work is by having a sacrificial lamb."

Troy looked at his brother with dissatisfaction. He and his twin brother were a lot of things, and Troy knew firsthand how cold-blooded Augustus was; this was a new low.

"I don't know, man," Troy said.

"The God these churches preach about, didn't he sacrifice his own son?" Augustus asked.

Troy looked on as the surgeons began to place the Nano-Hive into the boy's brain.

"His sacrifice was for the greater good."

"And if this works, just imagine how much good we can accomplish," Augustus replied.

You mean how much coin you can obtain. You're not fooling anyone, Augustus, Troy thought.

"Explain this to me one more time how this mechanism is supposed to work," Troy asked, shifting the conversation.

"The Nano-Hive has within it over a million Nano-Secs." Augustus paused, allowing it to sink in. "Once attached to any organism, it will completely take over that organism. So when the Nano-Hive attaches to my son's brain, it will release all the Nano-Secs throughout his body. But the kicker is that there is a beacon in the Nano-Hive that is going to command every Nano-Sec."

"How is it going to be commanded?"

"That depends on the boy. The goal is that the brain will receive a singular command that will register with the beacon, which will then send the message to the Nano-Secs."

"What command is the beacon looking for?"

"Anything along the lines of healing, increase in stamina and strength. Shit, a blind man could see again all based on a command. A paralyzed man can walk again. A pregnant woman's last breath can be a command to protect her baby while still in the womb. Imagine, Troy, a baby being protected by Nano-Secs while its host is completely dead."

Troy was impressed. Together they created a foundation that facilitated military contracts for weapons. But they were not the only ones in the game anymore. The competition was strident, and Augustus believed switching into pharmaceuticals was a better gambit; Troy didn't share Augustus's optimism.

"And if that command doesn't come?"

Augustus remained quiet as he pretended to take interest in his son's surgery.

———·—·———

Still Back in the Day

The pain was brutal for a seven-year-old. Miles knew the trainer wasn't using full force while training in hand-to-hand combat, but every punch felt like a brick hitting Miles. He did his best four times a week against his trainer. His father, Augustus, would observe every session emotionlessly, and Miles wanted nothing more than to impress him. Miles's mother thought differently. She believed a seven-year-old boy should be focused on being a boy. Her thinking usually ended with her aggressively arguing with Miles's father.

"Guard needs to be up, Miles," the trainer informed.

"I'm tired, Mr. Tracks," Miles responded.

Mr. Tracks looked up and saw an emotionless Mr. Augustus Graves. Augustus shook his head at Mr. Tracks, who knew that meant "Keep pressing the child."

"We still have another hour. Guard up. Let's go," Tracks said.

Tracks came and punched Miles, who tried to block it, but he got hit anyway. Tracks didn't stop; he grabbed Miles and tossed him around on the padded floor.

"Roll, boy, roll. Always assume the enemy is upon you," Tracks said as he caught Miles by his collar and threw him back to the ground. With little power, he kicked Miles in his ribs, but for a fragile seven-year-old, it felt like the worst pain in the world.

Tracks, a professional fighter-turned-coach, didn't enjoy his job beating up a little kid. But his influx of work quickly came to a halt due to his gambling debts. Tracks, in his arrogance, would bet on his fighters, and when they lost, he increased their weekly payments to coach them so he could make up for what he lost. His fighters figured him out, then ended up leaving him, and Tracks had to sell his gym to pay his debts.

It had been just another day. Tracks was doing his morning two-mile run when an all-white stretch transport cut him off. He was prepared to fight, but when he saw Mr. Augustus Graves step out, he had a change of heart. Long story short, Augustus offered him a job with a pay no one could refuse.

Tracks backslapped Miles hard, and he went down bleeding. This was the routine four times a week for the last two months—beat the boy. Tracks stood Miles up, smacked him in his face, and yelled at him with vulgar language before throwing him back to the floor.

"Every time I see you, I see a weak boy. How can someone like you ever make it in this world? You don't listen. You don't fight. You're nothing more than a paycheck to me," Tracks said, before laying more of a beatdown on Miles.

Miles looked up and saw his father sitting in a chair, his arms crossed, with a blank stare on his face. He wanted this training session to end, but he knew his father wasn't going to stop it anytime soon.

Miles grew frustrated. He didn't want to be here; he wanted to be back in his room playing with his fighter figures. His frustration switched to anger the more he thought about how his father always ignored him, how he wanted to impress him, but fighting wasn't it for Miles. He didn't even like to play wrestling with his older cousin, Styles.

"Get up and show me your guard, boy," Tracks demanded.

Miles stood up and did all he could to summon some willpower to take the hits. He imagined hard that he couldn't feel pain.

"You want to hit me, boy?"

I don't want to feel, Miles thought.

"Come hit me."

I don't want to feel pain. I don't want to feel your punches.

"Fuck it, I'll hit you then," Tracks said as he swung a backhand at Miles.

I don't want to feel anything! Miles thought hard.

Tracks hissed in pain as he rubbed the back of his hand. He was confused. He thought maybe he had hit the boy's teeth or something. He smacked him with an open palm, and it felt like slapping a metal pipe. Tracks stepped back, nursed his hand, and looked at Augustus, whose eyes were widening.

Augustus, a tall dark-skinned man with slicked-back wavy hair, looked at Miles and Tracks with new curiosity. Augustus gave Tracks the look to continue.

Miles was shocked and confused at why Tracks had hurt his hand, but his father had shifted in his seat. The first sign of any interest his father had during the training sessions. Miles's thoughts were cut short by a hard blow from Tracks's fist.

I don't want to feel pain. I don't want to feel pain, Miles thought through his dizziness.

Tracks saw Miles on all fours and decided to kick him. Tracks was not even in his forties yet, so when he saw the faint red hue that glowed on Miles's skin, he thought it was the lighting in the room, not an imparity of his vision. He proceeded with a kick.

"Ahhh!" Tracks yelled in pain as he fell to nurse his foot. "What the fuck? How are you doing that shit, kid?"

Augustus stood from his seat, his animation vibrant enough to knock the chair down. Miles's father had never acted in such a way, but Miles loved it. He stood and looked at Tracks. His young mind couldn't fathom what his father wanted him to do.

"Tracks, am I paying you good fucking coin to sit there and play with your foot? Do your fucking job, and don't you fucking dare hold back," Augustus's deep voice ordered.

Tracks stood, eager to make his wages, and came at Miles with balled fists.

Miles heard Tracks's bones break in his hand, and it was not pleasant.

Tracks cried aloud, and he gripped his hand. The more Tracks was in pain, the more his father was happy and showed interest in him. Miles saw Tracks sit down on the floor, nursing his hand. He saw his moment, and he took it.

Miles ran at Tracks, his seven-year-old battle scream filling the room. Miles balled his fist just like Tracks taught him and swung at Tracks's face, connecting a punch for the first time in two months. Tracks was not fazed by the blow and simply pushed Miles backward with little effort.

Miles came at him again. *Feel no pain.*

Tracks saw the faint red hue around Miles again, but there was no time to react.

Miles's fist felt like pure metal on Tracks's mouth. Tracks went down, bleeding, and Miles climbed on top of him and kept punching him. Miles was angry about these couple months of brutal training, getting kicked, punched, smacked, and yelled at.

He kept punching Tracks in his mouth. It wasn't until Augustus caught Miles's hand to halt him from his bloody onslaught that he stopped. Augustus looked at his son, who was sweating and breathing hard, his hands and shirt covered in Tracks's blood. Augustus felt nothing but joy, though his face didn't show it. He observed Miles's hands, which had no cuts or bruises, just bloody.

Present Day

Miles woke up from the memory with an agonizing headache. He tried standing, but his hands and feet were restrained to a chair. Bemused, he looked up to observe his surroundings, only to realize he was in a warehouse surrounded by a group of individuals wearing the same attire—black boots, black pants, zipped-up black jackets, black helmets covering their heads, and visors covering their eyes. Each one held a firearm and donned blue-and-yellow bandannas in their back pockets.

There was a taller man with a stylish hat, who was light-skinned with a tone, his arms covered in meaningless tattoos. He stood smoking some intoxicating substance.

"Where the fuck am I?" Miles asked.

"You don't ask no questions, chief," Lil P replied. "That be my job and my job only. If not, that's a shot."

"A shot?" Miles asked quizzically, deeply regretting the question when one of the individuals in all black came over and instantly shot him in the foot. But he had already activated his Flex, making the interrogation tactic null and void.

"The fuck?" Lil P said, confused. "Did you fucking miss or something?"

Lil P knew his subordinate didn't miss; he saw the whole thing. But based on what had just happened, he still couldn't believe it.

"What the fuck you want with the Loud 20s?" he asked Miles.

Miles looked at Lil P, noticing that there was nothing little about him. He was a tall son of a bitch, with an air of authority he wanted everyone to know that he had.

"I told you before. I speak to Jamal and Jamal only," Miles said.

Jamal strolled in, but Lil P intercepted him before he made his way over to Miles.

"Yo, we got a crazy situation here," he told Jamal.

Jamal peered behind Lil P's tall frame to see the man zip-tied to a metal chair, surrounded by his crew.

"What you mean?" he asked.

"Dude came out of nowhere and approached us, talking about he had a message for you."

"Where the fuck he press y'all at?"

"At Roxy's."

"The club motherfucker?"

"Man, he pressed us in the backroom. You know, where we store the young bitches before moving them."

Everything was registering with Jamal. How the fuck did anyone know about their side business at Roxy's? The only one with knowledge was Lil P, himself, the baroness, and Roxy.

"Don't Brandon big ass be watching the door?"

"That's what I am talking about," Lil P said. "He took Brandon out. Homie throat cut."

"Fuck." Jamal shook his head in disbelief. "How y'all get him here?"

Lil P looked back at Miles strapped to the chair.

"Young blood went to swing on him and ended up getting his own hand broken. We had someone sneak up behind him and piped his ass." Lil P made a swing motion. "He went down after that."

"OK, bet. Let me holla at him, see what's what."

Jamal walked over to Miles and sized him up, and Miles did likewise.

"OK," he said. "I'm here. What's the message?"

Miles sat quiet for a moment. He looked at the baron—middle-aged, dark-skinned with cornrows, fancy clothes, and jewelry.

"Your PDP is about to ring," he said. "You might want to answer it when it does."

"What you—" Jamal was cut off by the ringtone of his PDP. He looked at Miles, who nodded at him to answer it. Jamal noticed the caller ID—it was his baby momma.

"Yo, what? I told you I am dealing with something." A harsh voice came over the PDP. A ping came through for Jamal to accept the hologram mode his baby's mother was sending. He accepted on his end and saw a beautiful woman pointing a shotgun at his son's head.

"Miles," Rikii said.

There was an awkward silence. Jamal was shocked someone was holding his family hostage. Rikii broke the trance by shooting the TV screen in the bedroom.

"Miles!" Rikii shouted.

Jamal figured that was the man's name.

"Yeah, he's here," he said.

"Show me," Rikii instructed with her soft-toned voice.

Jamal moved his PDP to show Miles zip-tied to a metal chair. All the Loud 20s in the room saw Jamal's family being held hostage, the message clear—anyone can be touched.

"We got a deal?" Jamal asked as he signaled one of his men to cut Miles loose.

Rikii waited until Miles was free of his restraints before making her next move.

"Yeah, we got a deal," Rikii said as she aimed her shotgun at the woman and emptied a slug into her head, blood splattering all over her son. Rikii heard Jamal yell out, but she shot the PDP before any other word was said.

Jamal lost his mind. He ordered Miles to be shot, and his crew obliged. They emptied their firearms into Miles, who was rubbing his wrist from the zip ties. The bullets did nothing except leave holes in Miles's clothes.

Miles smiled at the fiasco attempt at killing him; he then quickly disarmed Jamal. The crew saw Miles had Jamal at a disadvantage and ceased fire. Miles threw Jamal's handgun across the warehouse floor, grabbed Jamal, and slammed him to the ground.

Miles got atop him and punched him in the face repeatedly. Blood splattered everywhere, but Miles didn't stop. He refused to relax his Flex and kept punching until there was nothing left of Jamal's face.

Lil P and the Loud 20s looked on in horror as they watched Miles stand, his face, clothes, and hands completely covered in blood. Miles looked over at the Loud 20s and pointed at a random person,

"You," Miles said, "come up here and take off your helmet."

The crew member did as he was told. He was young, dark-skinned with a militant haircut.

"What's your name?" Miles asked.

The young man looked at Miles's bloodied face and stared into his eyes, which was like staring into the abyss.

"Jared."

"Give me your firearm, Jared," Miles ordered.

Jared yielded, and Miles walked over to the members of the Loud 20s as he checked the rounds in the handgun.

"Y'all work for me now, and Jared here," Miles pointed back at Jared "will be the liaison between you and me." Miles walked toward Lil P. "And if anyone has a problem with the new hierarchy, well, that's a shot." He repeated what Lil P had told him earlier. He aimed his gun at Lil P's head and shot him. Lil P fell to the ground, lifeless.

5

Back in the Day

Miles stood in his bathroom, staring at his reflection in the mirror. He saw a young teenager with curly hair and little facial hair. Though most of the girls his age and some more experienced thought him handsome, Miles looked at himself in disgust. He couldn't stand the sight of himself, and he punched the mirror, shattering it to pieces. He went to his toilet and heaved; he had been puking all morning.

There was a knock at his bathroom door.

"Go away," Miles said.

"Open the door, boy." Augustus Graves's voice was commanding, low, and terrifying.

His father was the last person he wanted to see or talk to, but ignoring him would only mean bigger issues. He opened the door.

Augustus stood in Miles's bedroom, dressed in one of his expensive gray suits. The smell of his cologne made Miles want to puke even more.

"Why the hell have you not come down for breakfast?" Augustus asked. "Your mom and sister are already done eating."

"I don't feel well."

"Clearly." Augustus sized his son's lean body up and down and observed the glass all over the sink. "Well, what's wrong with you?"

Miles didn't want to talk about it, but he had no one else to talk to.

"The job went sideways, Dad," Miles said as he stood over the sink, looking at the broken glass.

"My reports said the bombing was a success."

"No, Dad. I mean, yes, the building blew but—"

"But what, boy?" Augustus's patience was wearing thin.

"I watched from the rooftop of another building. I used the scope on the sniper rifle to zoom in and made sure everyone that was supposed to show up to the meeting did before I blew it." Miles paused and forced his next words out. "I saw a kid, a little girl, probably six or seven, walk into the building. She had to be one of the politicians' kids or something." Miles waited, anticipating a lashing or a lecture. He hoped for an embrace, but he knew that was asking too much.

"So?"

"So?" Miles repeated back quizzically.

"Boy, life and death don't discriminate. They don't care how hard you have it or how easy. They don't sit around and handpick who is rich, pretty, ugly, or handicapped. They don't care, boy, so why should you? Control your emotions. Throwing temper tantrums is beneath us. Clean this shit up, get dressed, and go eat something," Augustus said, then took his leave.

———— • ————

Present Day

"Here is good, Rikii," Miles said as Rikii parked the transport and turned it off.

Miles sat in the back of the luxury transport and enjoyed the complimentary champagne. The news played from the TV on the window opposite him as he sat back with his feet up and fiddled through a box of cigars.

The news anchors went on and on about the war in Kurtaz.

"The sovereign supreme of Kurtaz says that he and the government are in one accord, that as long as their God is the ruler of all things, they will not bend their knees to any other, for God will protect Kurtaz and all the ancient cities within her," the reporter said.

Five other transports pulled up behind Miles, and people dressed in all-black outfits, biker helmets with visors, and blue-and-yellow bandannas hanging from their back pockets got out. Miles, disappointed to leave such comfort in a luxury transport, walked to the trunk to grab an old shotgun and a handgun. Rikii did likewise, except she grabbed a short-sized rapid-fire weapon.

A biker approached Miles with a PDP. He assured Miles all cameras would be disabled on his command, but Miles informed him that he wanted the cameras live. Jared stood, dressed the same as his peers, confused, because the only building of any promise in the area was a church across the street.

"You ready to do this, kid?" Miles spoke with excitement, like a child expecting to get into mischief with a friend.

"Are we going into the church?" Jared asked.

"Yes." Miles saw the confusion on Jared's face. "It's a trap house no matter how you look at it. From the man who is now inside there, pushing drugs to the man who stands behind a pulpit and leads lambs to their slaughter with fancy words."

Jared said nothing. Who was he to argue?

"Helmets on, y'all. Visors down," Miles ordered.

Miles and the Loud 20s crossed the street toward the church. From the outside, the church was brick, two stories high, and very aged. It wasn't the largest church, like the ones that enticed you with fancy glass, beautiful illumination, cushion seats, and the smell of fresh coffee with bagels. The parking lot was just cement with grass; no one cared about parking lines.

Miles, the only one not wearing a helmet, and the crew ran alongside the back of the brick church until they reached the rusty white double doors that had chains wrapped around the handles. A man approached the door with a pair of heavy-duty bolt cutters, and within a matter of seconds, they had access.

Miles stood directly in front of the door, while the others stacked on either side of the double doors, their shoulders against the church. The two men in front had their hands on the handles, waiting for Miles to give the signal to open the hordes of hell, and he did just that.

The package handlers were dealt with quickly because they were not armed. Six teenagers laid out, some who were eating still had fast food in their mouths. Miles and the group moved out of the kitchen and into the main hallway, not caring about the carnage they had left behind. They stood in the middle, and to their right was another hallway with classrooms on both sides, and at the end was a staircase. To their left was the entrance to the church, and in front of them were a few steps that led to big white double doors, which led to the pews.

Miles gave a signal for a few men to proceed down the hallway to the staircase. He watched them go as they tactically cleared every room, progressing down the hall. The remaining four proceeded to enter the pews. Only one of the white double doors were fully open, so they couldn't get a complete view of the pews. Miles reloaded his weapon with heavy cartridges and aimed it, ready once more to rain down terror. And then dread set in—heavy gunfire and the sounds of men dying came from down the hallway.

"Get down!" Miles shouted to his men.

Bullets from rapid-fire guns ripped through the walls, doors, and glass. A rain of fire came from the pews in overwhelming force. Miles never ducked or took cover; he relaxed his Flex and observed the damage. His comrades were dead; blood gushed from them as they lay on their backs, full of holes.

"Rikii?"

Without relaxing her Flex, Rikii touched Miles, signaling she was still there and unharmed.

Satisfied, Miles stepped over his subordinates, caring little for their lives, and proceeded into the pews. He shot a man, who was reloading in the middle of the aisle, in the head. Miles pumped his weapon and shot another, who was kneeling behind a bench, in the chest. He was now alone in the pews, unleashing Holy Hell on any who dared to show their face.

"Boss man, we clear over here," one of the crew members said while walking out of a room behind the pulpit.

Miles nodded and motioned Rikii to follow him. The room was another little hallway that held a private bathroom on the right side and had a staircase that led to the second floor, which was total carnage. Bodies lay everywhere between the Loud 20s and the occupants of the church, and blood covered the walls. Miles walked through the hallway, looking into what once were classrooms for kids. Books, toys, and crayons were spread everywhere and covered in blood.

Miles and Rikii, Flex relaxed, walked into the last room at the end of the hallway, where a man was still alive but wounded in his right leg.

The man sat against the wall in the corner, sweating and breathing heavily. The remaining Loud 20s stood around him, guns ready, looking fierce with their helmets on. The wounded man wore beige shorts, with white socks pulled to his knees and black slippers. His black tank top covered the myriad of tattoos he had on his yellow skin.

The classroom was slightly bigger than the others, which made it perfect for the two long metal tables in it. On these tables were powdered drugs wrapped in clear foil, blue-and-pink pills in mini bags, and duffel bags filled with eyedroppers and canisters with green liquid, which the new kids on the block are calling Juice.

Miles pulled up a plastic chair from a desk and sat in front of the injured man. The man sat, confused and in pain, as he clenched his right thigh and stared at Miles.

Miles used his fingers to make an invisible symbol of the cross over the man.

"You should be thankful. You have been blessed to survive this night." Miles scooted his chair closer to the injured man. "You're going to tell your baron that he works for me now. Let him know what happened here. Also, tell him I am a great boss. I don't accept quarterly fees, and all coins earned stay in his pocket. Tell him to call Jamal for a reference." Miles patted the man on his cheek and took his leave.

————— · —————

"I told you, I am not built nor equipped," the pale-skinned man said as he turned off the video of Bloody Hands disrupting his drug operation.

Roman sat and pondered aloud, "OK, so Bloody Hands is here in New Area, but why?"

The barons sat quietly. It was the baroness who broke the silence.

"I don't know why he's here, but he only asked us to do two things, and we would be square. He told us to stop paying quarterly fees to the Ryse. I assume it was to get the attention of the organization," she said.

"Oh, he most definitely got our attention," Roman said to the baroness. Roman leaned back in his chair, his legs crossed. "But what the fuck does he want?"

An uncomfortable silence filled the room the pale-skinned man sweating even more. The baroness took a shot of her drink and kept her eyes down. Jared, too, kept his eyes down. The Old Man was the only one who kept his composure. Roman read the room and knew something was off. He uncrossed his legs to prepare to leave.

"I believe you asked the wrong question." The Old Man's voice was low and raspy, but it was enough to keep Roman in his chair.

The Old Man leaned in close to Roman, who naturally leaned in as well to hear what he had to say.

"The question you should have asked was, what was the second thing he wanted us to do?" said the Old Man.

Roman sat puzzled, but before he could even get a word out, the garrote was wrapped around his throat. Rikii relaxed her Flex as she pulled tighter on the wire. Blood started to seep out of Roman's throat. He managed to stand up, but Rikii jumped and locked her legs around Roman's torso. Roman fell to the floor, his legs spasmodic, his clothes soaked with blood. He was finally still, and Rikii rolled off him. The door opened, and Miles walked through.

6

The baroness stood on top of the staircase, decked out in all-white glory, her brown skin glistening from rhinestones, perfectly decorated and positioned. Today she wore her diamond crown, which she'd personally designed, on top of her healthy and radiant Afro. Her makeup was done in a way that showed she was the one in charge, if you didn't already know by the crown.

She looked around at her gathering and noted affluent men and women dressed in all white, some wearing masks, dancing, and drinking. It was a celebration after all, for one of her girls managed to seduce a wealthy lawyer, and he'd paid her dowry. The baroness hadn't spared him, taking one of her girls from her stables was unheard of. However, the lawyer hadn't blinked an eye at the baroness's set price.

The classical music was roaring, the drinks were strong, and the baroness's boys and girls were out and about, seducing all who would give an inch. The baroness looked on, watching as her coins continued to grow. She thought back to how she'd made it to this point. She wouldn't say it was a struggle; all it took was just a little convincing of the world's weakest specimen—men.

She'd always had a sexual aura; she'd known it since she was a little girl. She used her abilities to seduce boys, and at first it started out as playful fun. She'd get boys to buy her candy or buy her a pop at school. But as she got older, her appetite grew, and so did her skillset.

She couldn't remember a time in high school when she lifted a pencil. She had teachers and principals under her heel, and if they misbehaved, well, videos would be sent to their wives.

College came, and she'd already broken a hundred hearts or so by then; two literally killed themselves. Her parents had known little of her activities. She'd always wanted them to view her as their little successful princess and made sure they never found out she used to dance at Roxy's three days out of the week. She had never danced just for the coin, which was for amateurs and poor women; she'd danced to stalk her prey, to have men fall for her, and then she would suck them dry.

Yet her appetite had continued to grow, and she needed new satisfaction. With her business degree, she worked for a couple of corporations. She was forced out of her first job in New Area for home-wrecking half the staff but managed to acquire a job at the Graves Foundation, where she seemed to get the most satisfaction, and there she met her match.

She first saw Augustus Graves when he was leaving a meeting and she walked past him in the hallway. Usually, all men stopped or gave her a second look, but not Graves. She took interest and decided to play a new game. She did all the digging she could on Mr. Graves and found out he had two kids by his late wife. His daughter, Tia Graves, was being groomed to inherit the company, while his son, Augustus Jr, was in and out of rehab for a drug addiction.

She studied Mr. Graves's schedule and deliberately tried to be in the vicinity of every meeting. She even asked her boss to allow her to sit in one of the meetings, which wasn't hard; her boss was a man after all. The baroness loved watching Mr. Graves, a man of power who sat and observed the room and spoke little. She made note of the tactic. If he spoke less and gave no insight on anything, it made the people uncomfortable. They should be uncomfortable; they were in a *Grave*yard.

The baroness sat at her desk, working on a project, when her boss called for her to meet him in a conference room. She didn't want to, but to keep her concessions, she had to do her part. The conference room held a long table with sixteen empty black rolling chairs and the view of the District of High-Top was incredible. But what made the view even more interesting was the woman who stood in the window looking over the district. Her burgundy business suit complemented her tan skin. Her body was desirable; she wore her clothes to fit her curves. Her gorgeous face made the baroness jealous. She wore her raven black hair in a braided ponytail. Her nails were well manicured, and they popped with design.

"Good morning," Tia Graves said as she turned to face the baroness.

"Morning, Ms. Graves. I was...um...meeting someone," the baroness responded, shocked and caught off guard for the first time in a long time.

"Your boss will not be attending this meeting," Tia said, "but I am curious why he held multiple meetings with you in a conference room instead of his office." Tia walked over and pulled a chair out for the baroness to sit in. She showed no emotion on her face.

"Sorry, I, um..." The baroness struggled to find the words.

"Listen, our company, our foundation, was not founded upon good merit. Though we achieved success, we evolved and moved into different avenues. Avenues that are extremely competitive, and right now we sit on the throne." Tia looked at Baroness, who sat still and focused. "Do you know what it means when you sit on the throne?"

"No, ma'am." The baroness's voice was low.

"Whoever sits on the throne has no friends, only enemies. So when our systems get flagged because an unknown user is looking into certain files or requesting to be in certain meetings and somehow always close by whenever my father is around, well, I get paranoid."

The baroness's heart sunk. She was so embarrassed and slightly frightened; Tia Graves did not give off an aura of kindness.

"So I looked into you to see if you're affiliated, and I was truly disappointed to see that you are not, and that the only thing you are is a whore. You will be escorted out of this building, and your belongings will be packed for you and sent to the address on file. If you come within a hundred feet of this building, I personally will fucking ruin you. Do you understand?"

The baroness began to answer, but two security guards came into the room and signaled her to stand up. She had to perform the walk of shame as they escorted her off her floor, down to the lobby, and out of the building.

The baroness soon found herself unemployed and back at Roxy's, dancing just to stay afloat. Roxy, an older yet ambitious woman, took note of the baroness' beauty and ushered her into her side business. Being in Roxy's stables was not ideal, but the baroness realized the power she gained in pleasing a man to the point when they tell their life stories, their business secrets, and their passwords—their loose lips always spilling out information. The baroness used this to her advantage, gathering information about investments and stocks.

She managed to seduce men who would help her grow her coin. Within a couple of years, she owned a few small businesses and had investments in other properties. She also learned that Roxy was in the hole with her club and decided to buy her out. Roxy was not happy, but she had no choice but to succumb to the shifting of powers. The baroness allowed Roxy to run the club, while she took on the side business and enhanced it. She had a successful run for three years until the Ryse came. They shifted the powers of New Area, and the baroness rose to even more power and title.

That brought her to now, standing at the top of the staircase. The crowd hushed as a couple strutted in. The baroness looked on with curiosity at the front doors to gauge the situation. The man was tall with two long braids reaching his shoulder blades, his skin bronze, his beard full and acutely lined. He donned an all-white fitted tuxedo with a black bow tie and dress shoes. The woman on his arm was dressed in a one-shoulder, modern white dress with a slit down the middle, revealing her left leg. She wore all-white laced-up heels, which completely complemented her legs and well-manicured toes. The baroness stood, taken aback by her beauty. The woman's pixie cut was styled with finger waves, her eyebrows naturally black, thick, and professionally arched. Her makeup was done to perfection, yet the baroness knew someone of her caliber didn't need much makeup.

The crowd drooled over her, and the baroness noticed her own staff were too stunned to approach the couple. But after a few short moments of admiration, the party continued, and people went back to their drinks and conversations. The baroness kept her eyes on the couple, who made their way to the bar. She decided to engage them because she had never seen them before.

"I must say, I've never, in all my days, seen someone make such an entrance," the baroness said, breaking the ice.

The woman looked at her and smiled but said nothing. The baroness looked over at the man, who paid neither one of them any attention.

"I didn't catch your names," she said.

Miles reached into his pocket, pulled out his PDP, and handed it to Rikii. Rikii fiddled with it for a second, pulled up a video, and handed it to the baroness.

"I'm your new boss," Miles said as the baroness held the PDP in her hand.

"Excuse me?" The baroness felt insulted.

"Press play, sweetie." Rikii gave the baroness a wink.

"And what is this video?" the baroness asked.

"Our understanding," Miles responded, still not looking at the baroness.

The baroness pressed play on the video and stood frozen; her eyes widened. She watched as her mother and father had their teeth violently removed. She watched her parents, lying unconscious inside of a trunk with bloodied rags in their mouths, get shot in their heads.

Rikii touched the baroness's arm in a comforting manner. "Do we have an understanding?"

The baroness was confused. Rikii's voice was of an angel, but she saw the devil in her hazel eyes.

"The fuck do y'all want?" she whispered angrily.

"An understanding," Miles said, finally looking at the baroness.

The classical music stopped, and the music became more alive as the guests started to dance.

"You want to dance, gorgeous?" Miles asked Rikii.

"You gonna take your eyes off me?" Rikii responded.

"Never." Miles smiled, grabbing Rikii's hand.

"Oh, I almost forgot," Miles said as he dug into his pocket and pulled out a small canister. He shook it, letting the rattling noise be heard. "This is for you." Miles handed the canister to the baroness.

The baroness took the canister and watched Miles and Rikii walk away to become the center of attention. They danced, grasping hands, their eyes locked on each other.

Rikii was fully aware of herself and knew her beauty rivaled the constellations. She knew she was not ordinary even when she was little. She understood God made a mistake, yet she did not buckle. She did not hesitate, for she was still perfect in every sense.

The music roared, and Rikii stepped back from Miles and started to rub her hands along her own body as if she was caressing herself for someone else's pleasure. The beat dropped, and she moved her hips from side to side.

She kept her eyes on Miles, who looked back at her as if she were the only one in the world. Rikii was conquering the dance floor. She moved her feet gracefully in her laced heels, and the guests gathered.

The crowd were more than impressed—they were mesmerized.

A random man, a little over six feet tall, bumped into Rikii, who seized the moment, grabbed him, took his hands, and put them on her waist as she grinded on him, still keeping her eyes on Miles. Rikii then crouched down and started bouncing her butt to the beat while holding the man's hands above her. Rikii noticed the quick glare of jealousy on the face of Miles, who recovered by smiling.

The crowd was loving it and focused their attention on Rikii. She once again took full advantage; she abandoned the stranger and went back to Miles. He reached out to touch her, but Rikii deliberately moved out of reach and stood behind a woman, the same as her height, who was dancing. When she noticed she was behind her she started to grind on her, feeling the music just as she was; Miles and the crowd were fully immersed. The woman picked up the pace by putting her hands on her knees and shook her butt on Rikii.

Sorry, mama. I'm in full control here, Rikii thought.

Rikii grabbed the woman by her hair to stand her up. She was in shock; she felt Rikii's privates for only a second until Rikii's soft hands caressed her breast, her throat, and her stomach. Rikii made her continue to grind on her, feeling more of her arousal. The woman tried to get Rikii's attention to kiss her, but tonight she was not her prey. Rikii abandoned her and went to Miles, throwing her arms around his neck.

Miles grabbed Rikii's waist, and together they moved back and forth. His mouth was parted, and they both felt each other's erection.

"You really like to get under my skin, don't you?" Miles laughed.

"That's not the only thing I like to get under." Rikii smiled as she glanced down at Miles's groin.

"What am I going to do with you?" Miles asked.

"Sandy beaches and fruity drinks," Rikii answered as she inserted her tongue into Miles's mouth.

The baroness was still shell-shocked at the video and even more so at the fact that the couple now gained the attention of all her guests with their promiscuous dancing. She finally came to and realized she had been holding the little metal canister that rattled every time she moved it. She unscrewed the top and immediately dropped the canister on the floor; the bloodied teeth inside scattering out.

7

Miles appeared through the door as if he was one with the shadows. He walked over to the lifeless body of Roman, whose angelic outfit was now blood red. He stepped over Roman, like one stepped over a curb, and approached the table full of barons.

"My need for you all is done. Do what you want." Miles looked back at Roman's lifeless body and back at the barons. "I will leave disposing of the body to you guys."

Sandy beaches and fruity drinks, Miles thought, reaching to lift Rikii up from the floor.

Miles took notice of Rikii's well-manicured hands that were now covered in Roman's blood. He reached his hand out to help Rikii stand. She grasped it, and together they walked out of the room and down the stairs, back to the club, leaving the barons in confused awe.

The music thumped, neon colors flickered, people drunk, dancing and spending coin. Miles pushed several people out of his way, still holding Rikii's hand. He made his way to the entrance of the club, noticing several men in suits guarding the door. He didn't recall them being there when he arrived. He paused, trusting his thirty years of experience. He turned to face Rikii and ushered her to make their way to the back of the club in hopes of leaving through the back exit. This time it was Rikii guiding Miles, hands still clasped.

Miles noticed Rikii's backside and couldn't resist squeezing it. He smacked Rikii's butt hard, making her stop, turn, and insert her tongue into his mouth. Miles gripped Rikii's butt with both hands and lifted her. Rikii instinctively wrapped her legs around Miles and continued her kissing. He enjoyed the kiss, but his eyes were open, observing the club. He saw more of the men in suits patrolling the bar to his left, a few others walking on the top tier of the club, and a couple more guarding the back exit. To make matters even more complicated, they all started to don gas masks.

"What you see?" Miles asked Rikii as he lowered her back down.

"Men in suits watching the crowd from the right. They're putting on gas masks," Rikii said into Miles's ear.

Miles paused to observe the situation.

"What you wanna do?" Rikii interrupted Miles's thoughts.

"We are going to just have to fight our way through. I have one fully loaded mag," Miles responded.

Rikii made a motion signaling Miles that she still had her switch-blade and garrote.

"You trust me?" Miles asked.

"I do." Rikii leaned into Miles. "You love me?"

Miles embraced Rikii, his eyes hungry for her. "I do."

Miles kissed Rikii hard and broke the embrace.

"We take the back exit," Miles informed Rikii.

"Alright, baby," Rikii said, still a little weak from the kiss.

Rikii tried to walk but stumbled and was caught by Miles.

"What's wrong?" he asked her.

"I don't know, baby. I'm dizzy as shit."

Miles started to feel the same way; he blamed it on the music and the cigarette smoke at first. But that wouldn't cause him to start sweating. He then felt like he had to vomit.

What the fuck? Miles thought.

Miles looked up at the ceiling of the club and remembered the men donning the gas masks.

They already gassed the fucking club.

Miles moved quickly and took out a handkerchief, covering Rikii's mouth and nose. He pushed himself and Rikii through the crowd to sit Rikii down. But the effort was cut short because of bullets being let loose from rapid fire rifles.

The Old Man sat at the table, observing the other barons; they sat quietly and very disturbed. He noticed the fat man in the cheap suit looking at him in the doorway and nodded to him.

Receiving the signal, the fat man spoke into his portable radio. "It's a go. Release the gases."

"Release what gases," the baroness asked as she happened to be ear hustling.

The Old Man didn't rush to answer but instead pushed his seat back and stood up.

"May your journeys be peaceful."

"The fuck that mean?" the pale-skinned baron asked.

His answer was a bullet to the back of his head. The fat man shot the baroness and Jared in their chest before they even registered what was happening.

"Jam the signals," the Old Man ordered.

The fat man took out his PDP and fiddled with it. "Signal has been jammed. No phone calls or messages will be sent out or received."

Twenty-two years he waited, twenty-two years of hurt he suffered. Moments like this never happen, and to be honest, he was not looking for this moment. But he always told himself if the moment ever came, he would not falter.

The Old Man had put his affairs in order. His son died from an overdose ten years prior, so he had no heir. He'd taken his coin and given each of his men one last bonus. He'd taken 2.5 million coins and donated them to the New Area authorities. He'd made sure the chief of authorities, who received a separate payment, understood that there was not to be any law enforcement presence at Roxy's tonight. The chief had explained to him that if shots or disturbances were reported, the Old Man would have ten uninterrupted minutes, and he didn't disagree.

The Old Man knew jamming the signals bought him a lot more time. The remainder of his coins he'd donated to charities across the Districts, and his paintings were to be donated to museums.

The fat man handed the Old Man a gas mask and proceeded to wait for further instructions. The Old Man closed his eyes and said a prayer aloud.

"May my loved ones continue to rest peacefully. I don't ask for forgiveness, nor do I ask for mercy. My punishments will be just, but take heed, no punishment is greater than me not seeing my family ever again. I ask for one thing—give me strength to rid the world of the cancer called Bloody Hands."

The Old Man looked at the fat man, who was already wearing his gas mask.

"EBGs—Everybody goes," he said.

The fat man walked outside the room and down the hallway that led secretly to the top tier of the club. The Old Man donned his mask, looking at the dead bodies that littered the room and thought only of sadness. Young men and women gone too soon, but their sacrifice along with others would save the lives of many innocents. The

Old Man's thoughts were interrupted by the screams of people dying from bullets being unleashed upon them.

Miles covered Rikii with his body as he absorbed the bullets from the rapid-fire weapons. He felt the pain throughout his body, which signaled him that his Flex was somehow weakening. He pushed Rikii roughly through the crowd of panicking people in a futile attempt to reach the exit. But that too was a fiasco; the men in suits blocking the doors were also shooting into the crowd.

The men in suits had all the top tier and both egresses manned with gunmen. Bodies were hitting the floor, and blood made the floors slippery, thus people began falling. Miles knew being on the floor was a death sentence. He also knew he was pinned and that this was no regular act of domestic terrorism. This was a premeditated act, and it was planned with tact.

Miles kept Rikii's head low; he couldn't let anything happen to her. There was nowhere for him to go. His only play was to continue to use his body to protect the love of his life and blend in with the crowd.

The shooting stopped, but people were passing out from the gases. Their panicking made them breathe more heavily, and they sucked up the gases like fruit punch. Miles guided Rikii to the bar and made her stay low.

"Listen! Move with the crowd and get the fuck out of here. I will find you," Miles said.

"The fuck you mean?" Rikii responded, frightened at the thought of leaving Miles. "I go where you go. You know this!"

"I can't get you out of here like this. I need to take the gunmen out. They'll be focused on me."

"No, Miles!"

Miles wrapped one hand around Rikii's jaw, the other on the back of her head, and kissed her hard, this time his eyes closed.

Everything around them was absent—no people, no music, no gunshots. It was just the two of them, their souls rejoining to form a union. Time slowed as their tongues greeted each other. Miles became animalistic, their kiss growing stronger. Rikii could feel Miles grunt and returned it with her own fierceness; their tongues battling. Loneliness is God's ultimate punishment, and Miles knew he deserved every ounce of it. Nowhere in the universe did Miles think he would love anyone or have anyone love him. What Rikii made Miles feel, he himself couldn't understand. He cherished Rikii. He adored her, and he would burn the heavens for her. He made sure Rikii felt all that he did in that kiss. Miles broke the trance that usually ended with very rough lovemaking.

"I will find you," Miles said as he held Rikii's face in his hands.

"Promise me."

"I promise."

Miles left Rikii's side and joined the fray of the panicking crowd. He took out his firearm and began shooting at the masked men in suits. He managed to kill two, which in turn had them firing back at him.

The crowd screamed and ran even more. Miles grabbed a random person and used him as a shield as the gunfire poured upon him from the top tier of the club. The innocent man was shot multiple times before Miles dropped him and shot at the gunmen. Miles didn't know if he hit any of them because he ran through the crowd as he was shooting.

Miles saw the gunmen who had been blocking the exit doors, making their way toward him. Miles deliberately blended in with the crowd, his black outfit being hidden due to the flashing neon lights. One of the men in gas masks had his rapid-fire weapon aimed at the ready. Miles grabbed the barrel of the weapon, pushing it aside as he kicked the man's knee.

The man went down, and Miles kneed him hard in the face, grabbing the weapon out of his grasp. The man's mask took most of the blow, but it didn't matter because Miles shot him anyway.

He aimed and shot a series of bullets at another masked man, killing him and a few innocents that were in proximity. Miles quickly took aim again at those on the top tier and began shooting. His aim was slightly off, the club was dark, and the gas was making him see double; he fought through it.

Miles pushed through the crowd to the exit, and fortunately, people managed to open the doors and escape the bloody madness. He pushed through the crowd but didn't notice one of the men in suits who had taken off his mask, making him unrecognizable. He tackled Miles to the ground. The man disarmed Miles and punched him in the face repeatedly. Miles, too weak to use his Flex, did his best to block the blows. The blows came to an end, and Miles noticed the man was pointing a firearm at him but not pulling the trigger.

The people were exiting the club, ignoring him and the man.

More gunmen came and surrounded Miles, and the man on top of him removed himself. Miles slowly stood up, woozy from the punches and the gas. The music was now shut off, and someone had the bright idea to suddenly turn on some of the lights. Miles saw clearly now, masked men in black suits and red ties pointing rapid-fire weapons at him. Some of the masked men were dragging the dead bodies out of the way, clearing the middle of the club.

"If you guys wanted to dance, all you had to do was ask." Miles smiled.

"Even in the face of inevitable defeat, you remain with your chest out and chin up," the Old Man said as he appeared from behind his men and removed his gas mask. "It finally comes to this, Bloody Hands."

8

"See, this is what I get for letting you fucking people live," Miles said aloud.

The Old Man was not fazed by the comment but instead signaled to his men. In unison all of his men took several steps backward, giving Miles and the Old Man plenty of room. A young man in a suit and gas mask ran up and stood next to the Old Man with his arms out. The Old Man removed his blazer, folded it, and laid it across the young man's arm. He undid his tie and laid it across too.

"Are you gonna kill me, or are we gonna fuck?" Miles asked impatiently.

The Old Man continued to master his emotions and ignored Miles, who observed the Old Man's body, which was covered in colorful tattoos, and beneath the art hid disciplined muscles. The Old Man finally removed his gloves and gave it to the young man, who ran back to where he'd been.

Miles, wearing designer dress shoes with slim-fit black slacks and an all-black short-sleeved collared shirt, received the message. He rolled his shoulders and rolled his neck. He knew he was in a precarious situation. He felt sick from the gas, his Flex would be of little use, and even if he killed the Old Man, the men in suits would just gun him down.

Fuck it. As long as Rikii made it out, that's all that is important.

The Old Man was quiet. He assumed his stance and signaled Miles to come at him.

"Oh, you got balls. But fine, let's get greasy," Miles said, approaching him.

Miles came at the man, swung a right hook and then a left; the Old Man ducked both and delivered a kick to the side of Miles's head. Miles caught the kick on his elbow and pressed him, throwing jabs, catching the man on the chin.

The Old Man was not fazed by the punch. For twenty-two years, he'd felt no pain. Miles came at him again, throwing a feint with his left fist and delivering a punch with his right. But the Old Man saw it coming and quickly kicked Miles in the stomach, stopping him.

The Old Man capitalized on the situation and swung his own series of fists at Miles.

Years of discipline, conditioning, training, and hardening his knuckles and shins allowed the Old Man to hit hard. Miles felt every blow; blood leaked from his face. Miles kept his guard and swung back. The Old Man ducked his right hook, grabbed Miles's right wrist, and went in for a single-leg takedown, allowing him to pick Miles up in a fireman's carry. He then threw Miles to the ground.

Miles got on all fours to recover, but the Old Man punted him in the face, causing blood to spurt everywhere. Miles rolled to his back, in pain. The Old Man stepped back, allowing Miles to stand up.

"The gas?" Miles slowly made his way to his feet. "You knew it was going to affect my Flex, huh?"

"Flex? Is that what you call that little ability of yours?" The Old Man held Miles in contempt. "I've been tracking you for the last two decades. I watched out for your work, and after conversing with the Loud 20s, I learned of your ability to absorb damage. I took a gambit on using this type of gas to help slow neuro functions. I'm glad to see that it worked."

"Ah, I see. I must have fucked you up back in the day. Please refresh my memory," Miles said, spitting some blood from his mouth.

"There is no need to dig up the dead. The only matter of importance is right now." The Old Man squared up once more.

Sandy beaches and fruity drinks.

Miles came at the Old Man and attempted a high roundhouse kick, but the Old Man dodged it and countered with a series of punches to Miles's ribs and finished with a right hook to Miles's jaw. The Old Man attempted a low kick to Miles's leg, and it landed. Miles stayed on his feet and circled the Old Man, who threw another kick to the leg, which also landed.

The Old Man took full control of Miles's lack of speed and slow reaction time by landing a third kick to Miles's leg and rushing in with a series of punches and then backing up.

Miles was wobbly.

The Old Man came at him again but with a flying knee, but Miles stepped out of the way to clear the hit and kicked the Old Man, who was unfazed by it. Miles squared up again and went to bear-hug the Old Man. Although Miles was forty-seven years old, he was still strong for his age, but the Old Man's strength was like wrestling a twenty-year-old. The Old Man broke the bear hug, but Miles immediately shot for a leg takedown, lifting the Old Man up and slamming him to the ground.

Miles fought through his fatigue and moved quickly. He circled to the front and put the Old Man in a front headlock but couldn't fully lock it in; he shifted to the Old Man's left side and delivered powerful knee shots to his ribs. He heard the Old Man grunt, finally delivering some pain to him. Miles hopped onto the Old Man's back to put him in a sleeper hold, locked his arms around the Old Man's throat, and hooked his feet around his torso. But with sheer willpower, the Old Man stood up with Miles on his back and ran into the bar countertop as hard as he could.

Miles felt every bit of pain on his back and loosened his grip on the sleeper hold. The Old Man broke free and swung a punch at Miles, who grabbed a beer bottle from the countertop and smashed it across the Old Man's face, halting his punch. Miles grabbed the Old Man and slammed his head on the countertop repeatedly. The Old Man fell to the ground and rolled out of the way, but Miles was on him and threw a series of punches, finishing with an uppercut to the body and an uppercut to the face. The Old Man went down, and now he, too, was bleeding.

The Old Man stood back up, and Miles grabbed him, dragged him, and threw him into the closest wall. Miles grabbed the Old Man by the back of his neck and pressed down as he delivered knee strikes. The Old Man blocked his face but felt the force of the knee strikes on his forearms. Miles stood him up to throw a punch, but the Old Man quickly ducked, went behind Miles, and picked him up, bringing him down to the ground hard. Miles sprawled to his stomach, and the Old Man threw punches to the back of Miles head before standing up. The Old Man stepped away, breathing hard; Miles stood up, struggling to stay on his feet.

I'm getting too old for this bullshit, Miles thought.

He faced the Old Man, who was running at him, this time landing the flying knee strike; Miles went down and didn't get back up.

———— · ————

Rikii was always different, not just her physical or sexual attributes but different. From the moment she was created, she had a sense of outdoing others. She wasn't the only one created for the work that needed to be done for the Graveses. There were plenty of other trainees that were trained and experimented on since birth. Rikii's Flex was not the strongest in the group, but it was efficient.

She labored harder than the others; she aimed to meet greater expectations in the eyes of her creator. But her physicality held her back, and the others knew it. She never was ashamed of her soft features, her inability to put on muscle, or her attraction to men. But her fellow trainees saw that the only way they could break Rikii was to shed light on those so-called imperfections. But they didn't realize what Rikii was; they didn't fathom that the serpent was still vicious, even if it had no legs or arms.

They never realized that Rikii was the project the whole time nor did they ever realize that they were nothing but mere food for Rikii; they learned that the hard way. Rikii had won a training exercise in the jungles of Rae, not far from their headquarters. She defeated and badly humiliated one of the other male trainees who had heckled her, verbally and physically abused her. She thought, when she returned to HQ, that she would finally earn the respect of the other trainees; she was wrong.

The others did not take Rikii's side; instead, they verbally bashed her. Rikii even overheard some of the trainees planning on replacing the rubber ammunition with real ammo so they could set up a friendly fire on Rikii. Rikii's victory during the training exercise had earned her extra coins on her monthly allowance, where she used to buy a well-designed switchblade.

Rikii spent the next few weeks sharpening her skills to be light on her feet while she used her Flex, and every night she sharpened her blade. One night, when all the trainees were sleeping heavily, she used her Flex and crept throughout the quarters, slitting their throats with her switchblade while they slept.

Tia Graves was amazed at the commitment of her creation. She expected nothing less, using the same playbook that her father used with Miles. Tia thought it best to increase Rikii's training, and in the end, Rikii became what she and Tia Graves always wanted—a perfect viper. And eight years ago, she was sent to do a mission with Miles and learn the tricks of the trade from him; well, that was what Miles was told.

———•———

The rage in Rikii's chest reached its pinnacle as she watched Miles go down. She stood in the shadow of the top tier of the club, donning a gas mask that she'd taken off one of the dead men in suits. It was useful, for Rikii was able to use her Flex a little bit easier. But judgment was nigh, and she removed her gas mask. She unsheathed her blade and crept slowly along the top tier of the club toward the men in suits. They saw their boss knock Miles out and thought it was safe to relax their weapons.

Fools.

Rikii approached the first of the men in suits and cut his Achilles heel, then slit his throat. Another suit saw what happened and took aim at Rikii, who threw her blade into the suit's eye. Rikii front-rolled and grabbed the rapid-fire weapon, shooting at the other suits on the top tier.

She ran and fired, hitting her targets with deadly accuracy. The suits on the bottom tier started shooting at the top tier, but Rikii took cover behind the second-tier bar. She breathed slowly to remain calm; she used her Flex.

The suits came up the stairs quickly. They saw their dead comrades and thought best to spread out, ten of them.

Two went to the bar and peered over. Seeing nothing but floor and alcohol bottles, they gave the signal that they were clear—idiots. Rikii was locked in and felt the bloodlust.

She relaxed her Flex and stood directly in front of a suit. She shot him but held him up with one arm and turned him to take the bullets from his comrades. She Flexed again, dropped the dead suit and weapon, and ran to another suit.

Rikii jumped and used her legs to wrap around the head of the suit. She used her momentum and agile body to flip the suit. She quickly grabbed the rapid-fire weapon and began shooting at the remaining suits. Rikii dropped three of them, leaving five.

The suits shot aimlessly because they couldn't pinpoint Rikii; all they could do was hope. Someone must have been looking out for Rikii because they all ran out of ammo and needed to reload. Rikii shot and killed two suits before her mag went empty. She ran to the suits and swung the gun at the head of one of them, who fell hard. The other suit was wise to duck Rikii's swing. The suit tried to grab the gun. Rikii let him. kicked him in his groin, and quickly got behind him, wrapping the garrote around his throat.

The last suit completed his reload and aimed at Rikii. She swung around in time, leaving his comrade to empty his rounds into his partner. The dead man fell, and no one was behind him. The suit started shooting at the air, panicking because he couldn't locate Rikii. She relaxed her Flex and screamed as she charged the suit. She was able to move the barrel away from him, but the suit was physically stronger. Rikii didn't care. She tried to wrestle the gun away. The suit punched Rikii, who dodged it and forced the suit backward. He stumbled on his feet, and he fell, taking Rikii with him.

Still managing to keep the barrel away, she punched the suit repeatedly in the face. The suit was able, through brute strength, to toss Rikii off him. She sprawled to her knees and quickly kicked the suit in the face. She dove for the gun that he'd dropped, but the suit was also able to dive for it. Rikii grabbed a handful of the suit's neatly combed black hair and slammed his face down onto the floor, breaking his nose. The suit still had one hand on the gun and used the other to hit Rikii; this time it landed, but Rikii didn't let up.

She managed to get her finger onto the trigger and fired, bullets shot off haphazardly clearing the magazine fully. The suit, his face bloodied, stood up, and Rikii did likewise. Rikii came at him swinging. She landed a hit, but the suit took the punch. He grabbed Rikii by her clothes, and she took hold of him. She grabbed a handful of clothing under the suit's right arm and his left collar. She quickly leapt, placing her right leg into the suit's midsection and her left leg around the right side of the suit's head. She leaned back and lifted her hips with all her strength. Rikii felt the suit's elbow pop, and he yelled in pain. She released him and watched as he kneeled down to nurse his elbow.

Showing no mercy, Rikii stood behind the suit and snapped his neck.

Rikii ran to the stairs, where more suits were coming up. She Flexed and handled the first suit on the top step. She took the barrel of the gun and aimed it up, and then kicked the man in his stomach, making him and his comrades tumble down the stairs.

She ran down the stairs. The first man to get up received a hard punch to his throat. The second tried to shoot but didn't know what to shoot at.

Rikii grabbed the man struggling for air and threw him back down the stairs. The distraction was enough to disarm another suit, and Rikii began shooting the remaining suits.

What they didn't understand about Rikii was that they thought the threat was Miles. Shots rang out as the remaining suits spread out on the bottom tier of the club. They didn't know they were facing the woman who was created for one sole purpose—to replace Bloody Hands.

— · —

Back in the Day

"All right, playboy, you done here," the barber said as he spun the chair around so that Miles could see himself.

The barbershop was not big, but it was efficient enough to hold four barbers who had a good flux of clientele. The popcorn ceiling showed its age, with yellow stains from years of water damage and possible other issues, and the floors were cracked white tiles that needed to be replaced. The barber chairs themselves had seen better days, but their rips, tears, and stains all added to the customers' comfort. An ugly barber chair showed that the barber had been around for a while and had wisdom with the clippers that a younger generation could not fathom.

Miles, sixteen, had begun to become aware of himself, and his presentation was everything to him. His dad would give him a fair amount of coin after he completed his tasks, and with quickness, Miles would spend it on new designer clothes and sneakers. But one thing was for sure, his haircuts were top priority. Miles saw that the barber had given him an all-around fade and left his hair curly at the top, his line up sharp.

"Yeah, that will do it, Slick," Miles responded.

Slick had been Miles's barber for about a year; he came recommended by Miles's uncle, who used him periodically. Slick was an older man, his beard fully gray, head cleanly shaven, and he dressed professionally. He always wore dress clothes to the shop and had no problems rolling up his sleeves, his arms decorated in tattoos, for his eight-to-ten-hour shift. Slick wasn't the only man of age in the shop.

The other three were roughly the same age, and their skill paralleled one another, so it didn't matter whose chair you sat in—you were going to get a clean cut regardless.

"The usual price, playboy," Slick said.

"What you say, about another couple months we can work on connecting this beard?" Miles asked as he paid Slick his coin.

"Slow yo roll, playa. Enjoy the baby face because, trust me, once the razor bumps come, it hurts like child support."

"What you mean by that?"

Slick laughed. "Just enjoy being a youngin, playboy."

Miles shook Slick's hands, exited the barbershop, and walked to the all-white stretch transport that had been parked outside the shop. A tall dark-skinned gentleman dressed in a tuxedo stood by the passenger end of the transport and opened the door for Miles. Inside the transport was top tier—sunroof, heated and cooling seats, and within the floor, there was a device that projected holographic movies and shows.

"Everything good?" Augustus asked as Miles sat down.

"Yes, sir," Miles said, looking at his reflection on the window so he could play with his hair.

Augustus watched his son and tried to remember a time when he was so self-absorbed in his young age; unfortunately, his mind drew a blank.

"I need to stay looking fly, Pops," Miles said.

Augustus ignored the statement.

"I got a spell tonight," Miles said as he checked his sneakers for any sign of blemish.

"You have to spell what tonight?"

"Jeez, I can't with you old folks. I have a date tonight. Me and this girl are going to the cinema to see some new movie that I am praying isn't a chick flick."

Augustus leaned back into his seat and played on his PDP, ignoring Miles.

Oh, what's the girl's name? How did you meet her? Would she be someone your mother would approve of? You know, Pops, these are simple questions that you can ask if you weren't so much of an asshole, Miles thought.

Miles watched his father completely ignore his presence, and Miles felt ill. He knew his pops would never speak to him like he saw other dads speak to their sons, but he still wanted to engage him somehow.

"What cinema did you and Mom go see a movie on your first date?"

Augustus looked and saw that his son was trying to make conversation with him, so he took the opportunity to educate him. Augustus pressed a button, rolling up the partition divider that separated them from the driver, now making their part of the transport soundproof. The driver, apt in his job, turned the radio up and stayed focused on the road.

Must have been one hell of a cinema, Miles thought.

"When I was younger, I met a man. This man spoke to me like a normal man. He looked like a normal man, but he was not a normal man. I cut him. He bled, but pain did not register on his face. I stabbed him in the heart, but he did not die. Shit, he didn't even fall. I fought him further, and he was always a step ahead of me. When I thought I could catch him off guard, he showed me his strength and durability."

Miles was mesmerized that his dad was actually speaking and didn't mind if the story was bullshit or not. "How did you beat him then?"

Augustus paused as if he was too ashamed to answer his son's question.

"Later on I found out that man was a creature of metallic build, but his mind and conscience was human. It was revealed that they call themselves Shifters, a fitting name. You ever come across a shifter? You fucking run. You run for the hills. You are nowhere near ready to fight one, boy."

9

Rikii leaned against the wall, a rapid-fire weapon aimed at the ready.

Death comes for us all, she thought.

The remaining men in suits had spread out and had her pinned. She could take at least two or three with her, but sadness had set in her heart. Not for fear of death but for parting with Miles under such circumstances. She saw Miles still on the floor, trying to recuperate from his defeat.

You are my world, and I will find you in the next life, Rikii thought as she took one last look at her lover.

The suits had spread out, rapid-fire weapons aimed at Rikii. They waited for the signal from the Old Man to put Rikii down for good.

A suit was suddenly snatched from where he was standing and was sucked into the shadows of the club. His quick yelp and the drop of his weapon sprung his comrades to point their weapons with one accord in the direction of the noise.

There was silence, then they heard something tearing and something spilling.

The Old Man, also intrigued, abandoned watching Miles struggle to one knee and Rikii.

Rikii took full advantage of the distraction and crept to Miles. Her steps were halted when she saw the head of a suit being rolled like a bowling ball back toward his comrades. The suits looked at the lifeless head, his dead face painted with shock and horror. They didn't wait for any signal; they unloaded their magazines into the area where the head rolled from.

The bullets stopped, the barrels of rapid-fire weapons were smoking, and sweat poured down the faces of the suits. Slow footsteps came toward them, and Roman appeared from the shadows. His throat showed the cut from the garrote, blood staining his neck and his all-white outfit. Bullet holes newly decorated his attire, yet he walked feeling no effects.

Roman, his face shifting in and out from human form to a scaled metallic form, looked around and analyzed the club. He saw Miles on one knee, struggling. He saw the Old Man, who stood defiant, and scared young men pointing empty rapid-fire weapons at him. Dead bodies and blood spread throughout the club, and finally his eyes fell upon Rikii.

"That was a cute party trick," Roman said to Rikii. "Want to see mine?"

Roman moved with inhuman speed toward the suits. He swung a right hook at a suit so hard it completely took the young man's jaw off; he died instantly. Wasting no time, he grabbed another suit by the throat and slammed him to the floor. Roman finished him by stomping his foot on the man's face, squashing it.

Another suit couldn't reload his weapon in time, so he swung it at Roman's head, which caught it. He tried to remove the gun from Roman's head, but Roman didn't move. The young man tried to punch Roman, but he caught his fist and tightened his grip on both the weapon and fist, slowly crushing metal and bone. The young man screamed in pain and pleaded for mercy; it didn't come. Roman squashed the young man's hand and weapon. Blood squirted from his hand, and within a second, Roman released both hand and weapon, grabbed the young man by the throat, and ripped out his Adam's apple.

Miles looked on. He wasn't shocked at the sight, nothing new to his eyes. He worked through his increasing headache and body fatigue; Rikii came to his side to try and help him up.

"Get out of here," Miles said through painful breaths, looking at Rikii with pleading eyes.

"Fuck you," Rikii responded.

Roman finished dismembering the remaining suits, leaving the Old Man the last one standing.

"What are you?" The Old Man asked.

"He's a fucking shifter." Miles volunteered his knowledge.

"What the hell is a shifter?" Rikii asked, and the Old Man also shared Rikii's cluelessness.

"It's something we don't want to fuck with," Miles said.

"Bloody Hands." Roman's voice no longer no longer sounded like that of a human, more like computerized. "I haven't seen you since Euphoria. I remember the massacre of Scotts Beach all too well. All those investors and their families gone, and what happened to the people of that island? A shame, really."

"Yeah, jack, I don't fucking know you," said Miles.

"You wouldn't remember. The bodies on your hands are like grains of sand." Roman made eye contact with the Old Man. "And you, Jean, I'm amazed at the lengths you would go to kill Bloody Hands." Roman looked around the club. "So much carnage, and for what Jean? For what?"

The Old Man mastered his emotions despite a computerized voice saying his name and questioning his reasoning.

"He murdered my wife," he told Roman.

Roman laughed, not a pleasing sound from a Shifter. "Who? Him?" Roman pointed at Miles. "You did all this because he killed your wife?"

"I don't see the humor in it," Jean responded calmly.

"Well, of course you wouldn't. You spent two decades thinking it was Bloody Hands who killed your Lauren," Roman said.

Jean looked at Roman, confused, his heart beating fast. "What do you mean I *thought*? And how do you know my late wife?"

"Jean, she's dead because of you." Roman let the comment sink in. "You don't remember your transgression?" Roman saw the puzzled expression on Jean's face, which now seemed older. "Goodchild. He set you up for failure."

Jean sprung at Roman, his composure now gone. Roman easily maneuvered away from Jean's strikes.

"Goodchild was warned about the lands in Rae. He was ordered to stand down." Roman knocked Jean to the ground. "But he was too privileged to be told no. So we attempted to kill him, but he miraculously survived the heart attack."

Jean rose, but Roman kicked him back down. "His ambitious young assistant thought he could make a name for himself by trying to finish what Goodchild started," Roman said.

"We didn't see you as a threat, Jean, but you fooled us, didn't you?" Roman grabbed Jean and threw him across the club effortlessly.

"You hired the best private investigating team. And what did they find, Jean?" Roman stalked Jean, who was crawling on the floor, then stepped on his hand, breaking the bones.

"What did they find, Jean?"

The Old Man looked up at the bloody machine. "IBN"

"Say it again for the people in the back." Roman stepped harder on Jean's hand.

"IBN! International Banking Network!" Jean shouted through the pain. "It was a shell company being used to purchase the lands."

Roman aggressively picked Jean off the floor. "What else did you find, Jean?"

Through pain and old age, Jean forced himself to remember fine details from two decades ago.

"We tracked the company's finances. We discovered the shell company was being used to illegally collect coin throughout the Districts' criminal enterprises and was being disbursed to finance certain parties who were involved in the Water Wars," Jean said.

"Yes, do you see now, Jean?" Roman said, punching Jean in the stomach. Though it was light, it was enough to drop the well-conditioned Old Man. "Bringing to light what we were doing, well, we lost a lot of connections and investors. Ryse was brought low, and that is unacceptable, Jean. Over a century of networking, damn near destroyed because one little asshole wanted to make a name for himself." Roman put his foot on Jean's neck. "That disrespect couldn't go unanswered."

Jean knew what was coming next. He hadn't realized it before, never connected the dots. To think the man who was the most feared throughout the world was responsible, it was the most sensible explanation. Especially since in the end, the Graves Foundation won the bidding. It only made sense it was the Graveses who killed Lauren to keep him from signing on the dotted line. But he was wrong. He'd allowed his son to die alone with a needle in his arm. He'd killed so many people in anger. Tonight he had massacred innocents to kill a man who was not even responsible for any of his transgressions. Jean lay on his stomach. He could only look at the dead bodies around him while death came for him.

"Forgive me," Jean whispered to himself, hoping the innocent lives that were taken this night heard him.

"We killed your wife," Roman said as he broke Jean's neck.

10

"So is that what Kurtaz is all about, huh?" Miles asked aloud. "Ryse using the same methods as before to finance the Invaders."

Roman stepped away from Jean's lifeless body and made his way to Miles and Rikii.

"Exactly, hence you're reasoning for being here," Roman said.

"What you want in Kurtaz?" Miles asked.

"We want Rae. And because the Graveses are unmovable, well, we had to take other drastic measures. Come to think of it, the war might soon come to an end. Either we lose for lack of financing or we win. But me obtaining Miles 'Bloody Hands' Graves would absolutely make the Graveses movable."

Miles was not affected by Roman knowing his identity, but he knew he would be damned if he let anything happen to Rikii.

"I'll come freely," he said. "You let Rikii walk away unharmed."

"You got me fucked up if you thinking I'm leaving you," Rikii said.

Roman, his face still shifting from form to form, rubbed his throat where Rikii had used the garrote. "It's hard for me to forgive such a—"

The authorities burst through the door, interrupting Roman.

"Get the fuck on the floor all of you now!" yelled the authorities, dressed in all-black tactical gear, which included useless body armor and helmets, with weapons aimed at the ready.

Roman turned to face them, and to no one's surprise, they fired upon him.

Miles watched Roman take the bullets and then began to dismember their whole team. Miles grabbed Rikii by the hand, and like two high school sweethearts trying to escape the rain, they ran. He led Rikii to the back of the club, through the kitchen to another exit. The sounds of more bullets and men dying echoed as Miles and Rikii exited the club. They ran through the alleyway, into the street, Miles getting a burst of well-needed energy. He stopped the first transport he saw and roughly removed the driver.

"I'm driving," Rikii declared; Miles didn't argue.

Rikii sped off, ignoring all traffic laws.

"Well, I ain't see any of that coming," Miles admitted.

"Yeah, no shit," Rikii replied with a hint of disappointment in her voice.

"You're mad at me for that?"

Rikii zipped in and out lanes. "No."

"What is it then?"

"I don't appreciate you always trying to get rid of me!" Rikii made a hard sharp turn, making Miles fall into his passenger side door.

"I was just looking out for you."

"I don't care, Miles! We fight together. We win together. We even lose together, even if that means dying. We do it together."

Miles paused for a moment. He looked over at Rikii, her features still benevolent despite blood and some bruising on her face.

"What? Why are you looking at me like that, Miles?" Rikii shot a side-glance at him.

"I'm sorry, Rikii."

"For what?" Rikii asked, but Miles didn't answer. She quickly looked at Miles, whose eyes were barely open.

"Miles! Miles!" Rikii yelled and shook him. Miles's stomach was bleeding; he had taken a stray bullet from the authorities.

"No! No! You motherfucker!" Rikii pulled the transport over. "Wake the fuck up, baby, please. Miles, stay with me. Sandy beaches, fruity drinks, remember?" Rikii smacked Miles hard.

His eyes fluttered open.

"What I say?" She yelled at him. "We die together. If you go, I swear I will drive right into the fucking river, Miles. Fucking try me. You want me to fucking die, Miles?" Rikii screamed at Miles, her eyes red and tears running down her cheeks.

Miles heard Rikii screaming, but he couldn't see anything, everything was going black.

Fuck me, this is how I go, huh? Miles pictured the beach, him and Rikii in their beach chairs, their feet dug into the sand. Their hands were clasped as they drank their favorite drinks. Miles saw it all—him holding Rikii in the ocean, her legs wrapped around him, their lips greeting each other.

Damn, I was so close.

Rikii sat emotionless. She could do nothing but look at Miles's dead, battered body. Eight years of memories, eight years of nothing but love and bliss. Eight of the best years Rikii knew she would ever have. She thought back to the first time they'd made love, both were too scared to touch each other. It was Rikii who initiated, kissing Miles's hand. It turned into Miles caressing Rikii's face and drawing her close to him. Both feeling each other's hardness, Miles stripped Rikii, and Rikii did likewise to Miles.

There they stood, under the night sky, the moon waiting to witness their union. Miles started to kiss Rikii, but she pulled back, making Miles chase her a bit. Miles smiled and kissed her hard. Their kiss became sloppy and passionate. He grabbed Rikii by her privates and stroked her. Miles watched Rikii's beautiful, thick arched eyebrows lift as her eyes rolled to the back of her head. He turned Rikii around so he could stand behind her, leaned down, kissed Rikii's neck, and caressed her small breasts, exciting her even further. Rikii reached around and caressed Miles's manhood, enjoying the sound of his breathing. Rikii motioned to Miles that she wanted to break the embrace. Miles faced Rikii, confused, but she winked at him and got on her knees. Rikii, never breaking eye contact with Miles, took Miles into her mouth. She felt Miles's legs weaken and took it as a good sign. After a few minutes of pleasure, Rikii lay on the blanket with her legs spread, indicating Miles to lay on top of her, and he obliged.

———•·•———

The bar was filled with silent whispers and despair. People sat or stood, drinking their depressions away, and Miles was no different. He knew death came for everyone, and he always knew his fate; it was never the pearly gates for him. He accepted his death as he sat at the counter, drinking a whole bottle of the strongest liquor the venue had to offer. He sat, dressed in an expensive designer tuxedo, his hair neatly braided and beard trimmed.

"How's the drink?" The woman's voice was soothing as she sat down next to Miles. She wore an all-black dress; her features were beautiful. Her hair, black and kinky, fell past her shoulders.

"It would taste better if I wasn't being bothered," Miles responded, not even looking in the woman's direction.

"At first there's confusion, not knowing where you are and not knowing what comes next. Then comes worry, worrying about the ones you left behind, and then there is regret, thinking about all the things you could change. So which one is it that you're feeling right now? And don't answer confusion because, like most people here, they knew they were coming."

She ordered herself a drink.

Miles peered over at her, disgust on his face, but he remained silent and returned to his drink.

"Ah, so its regret then," the woman answered. "It's a shame, really. I genuinely feel bad for you. To go so long with no love in your heart, for it to finally bloom, and just like that," the woman snapped her fingers, "it's gone from you."

"What do you want from me?" Miles asked.

"Nothing. I'm just here to make sure you're comfortable."

"Ah, I see you're here to usher me, and because I only have one loved one currently dead, you thought it wise to wear my mother's face."

"Well, did it help?" The woman looked at Miles with genuine concern.

"No."

The woman moved closer to Miles.

"What if I told you that I can send you back?"

Miles looked at the woman, who was now uncomfortably close.

"If you expect me to beg, don't get your hopes up."

"Not even for Rikii? You wouldn't beg?" The woman asked, making a puppy dog face.

Miles knew damn well he would beg, bark like a dog, and run through the streets naked to be back with Rikii, and the woman knew it too; she saw through his facade.

"Is that what you want me to do?"

"Not at all," the woman said. She mysteriously pulled out an envelope decorated with unique designs and lettering of a language not known to man.

"You people have no idea how realms work. You all speak of a devil of some sort and a savior. And all that is fine because all that is accurate in some other realm. But history was lost, and no one searched to understand the original playbook. There is no devil here. There is no savior," she said. "You want to go back. Well, in that envelope is, um, how do you say it? Our understanding."

Miles opened the envelope and found a piece of ancient parchment that was wrinkled and blank.

"There is nothing written on it."

"I know. That's the deal. Are you willing to sign your name not knowing what I have in store for you? Is Rikii worth that much?"

———— · ————

The rain came heavy, the drops hitting the transport like little bombs. Rikii couldn't bring herself to move just yet. Still stuck in the entanglement of memories, she felt pain and sorrow wrecking her heart. Rikii leaned over and caressed Miles's face. She ran her fingers through his braided hair. Her thumbs caressed his eyebrows. Tears ran down her face. She had her whole life ahead of her, but her world was gone. She wouldn't know how to handle life without the man she had given her soul to. She gave in and kissed Miles on his lips for the last time, finally letting out the remaining of her tears. She felt Miles's tongue kiss her back, and she was stuck in the embrace. Rikii jumped back in shock and looked at Miles, who tried to sit up. Rikii grabbed Miles by the jaw, her grip strong. She stared into his eyes. Miles grabbed her hand and felt her shaking from the nervous breakdown she was about to have.

Miles stared at her for a moment.

"Hell can't have me just yet. I still belong to you," Miles said.

Rikii's eyes watered even more. "Don't ever do that to me again. You fucking promise me."

"I promise."

"Sandy beaches and fruity drinks?" Rikii asked.

"Sandy beaches and fruity drinks," Miles said. "OK, maybe the hospital first." He coughed.

Rikii kissed Miles, and together they were on another plane. The rain fell upon them as they gazed upon each other's countenance. The trees bore testimony to their passion. The stars formed perfect constellations, for it was their crowns. The moon had radiated them, for it was their glory. The wind was beneath their feet. They moved to the beat of their own orchestra, their hearts becoming one, fulfilling their passions till the universe said they were done.

Rikii pulled away from the kiss and looked into Miles's eyes, both hungry for another, both in unison of what they just felt.

———— · ————

The rain carried the dead people's blood down the streets. Roman stood outside, in between the transports of the authorities, their dismembered bodies surrounding him. He looked down the streets of New Area and thought better about chasing Bloody Hands.

"We are going to have our dance one day, Bloody Hands, for Ryse there are many, and our reach knows no bounds," he said aloud.

Roman turned and leapt up onto the building, disappearing into the night sky.

———— · ————

Way, Way, Way Back in the Day

Grool the Giant stood at 7 feet 5 inches; he was 350 pounds of pure muscle. His body was covered in a chalky substance that prevented him and his people from being located through their heat signatures. His head was bald, his earlobes filled with piercings, and tattoos covered his thick forearms. He had decorated his wrists with metallic bracelets. He wore a type of animal fur around his waist. His legs were monstrous. His appearance was dreadful, and his weapon, a heavy axe, made him look more hellish. He stood with his people, looking into the sky at the Great Ark.

Buddha Bane, I see death is at my door, and I am the fool who sent it an invitation, Grool thought.

Weeks prior, a group of messengers were sent to Grool's lands to inform him he was being evicted from the place where he and his people lived for generations. The royalties wanted the land to continue to expand their empire and replace Grool's trees and grass with their monuments, buildings, and paved roads. Grool's answer to that was removing the heads of the messengers and returning them to the sender.

The Great Ark, at least three hundred yards long and wide, hovered in the air, descending the sky. A great blue illumination descended from the Ark and engulfed the ground, blinding all who looked upon it. The illumination lasted for five minutes before disappearing, leaving a platoon of warriors in its place. The warriors were fierce, their black suits and helmets padded with metal plates, and their weapons, long blades, and metal shields materialized from a mechanism on their forearms. Their black capes blew in the wind, identifying they were of the royal military.

The military formed a hole in their ranks as a man walked through. He wore no suit and no armor, but he was dressed in an unbuttoned, gray trench coat that revealed a black body suit, which was decorated with haphazard metallic designs, and he donned high-legged black boots. He was a tall, muscular man, his skin dark, his hair long and wavy and tied back. He walked past the warriors and met Grool, who was standing out in the field with his people behind him, their spears ready.

Grool was shook with disgust; he hated technology. His people lived off the land and free from the rule of kings, queens, and politics for generations. His people and his Klan were in his charge, and he had a duty to see that their way of life is preserved, no matter the cost, no matter how great the sacrifice.

"Grool, Son of No One," Buddha Bane taunted as he approached the giant.

"Buddha Bane, Death Bringer, Blessed Son of the Gods, I say what a pleasure," Grool responded.

"Ah, so even my titles reach those who live in trees and shit in bushes," Buddha insulted. "This could have been avoided."

"Agreed. All you had to do was leave us in peace."

"I'm low in the hierarchy. Who am I to make decisions? Their will shall be done."

Grool let his great axe rest upon his shoulder. "And their will is to rid my people of their home. We have been here for generations."

"They were messengers, Grool. Killing them is a violation." Buddha looked to the sky, irritated, and back at Grool. "I am pretty sure you and your people can find other lands."

"These lands are our home."

"Not anymore."

It had been tradition since the days of old, if two parties wanted to avoid massive bloodshed, a duel shall be held. Buddha removed his trench coat, letting it hit the ground. The haphazard metallic designs on his clothes began moving, nanotechnology that formed an armor around Buddha. It was what years of victories got you to be granted by the king or queen, the title Lord of War. You were gifted with a Nano-Suit that sparked fear into enemies. Buddha was now donned in heavy steel armor, his arms now plated with steel, his shoulders bulky from the layered steel work. His breastplate bulky and faulds wrapped around his waist, steel formed even on his legs. To opponents, the armor looked way too heavy to maneuver in, but with the nanotechnology, Buddha felt light as a feather.

"May death be easy upon you," Buddha said as the nanotechnology formed a helmet that covered his whole head and face, only his eyes visible.

A young warrior from Buddha's rank held his sword within its scabbard beside him. Buddha unsheathed it, relishing in the beauty of its craftsmanship. The black handle of the blade was long enough to grip with both hands and had a ruby within its pommel. Its cross guard held the sword's lengthy double-edged blade that shined and was thoroughly wetted.

Grool the Giant wasted no time and charged; he swung his axe in an uppercut maneuver, hoping to cut through Buddha's steel plates. Buddha displayed great athleticism as he dodged the attack. He tried to stand out of Grool's range to assess his options, but Grool was fast. As soon as he saw his attempt fail, he recovered and brought the axe from above his head, downward. Buddha anticipated this and rolled away to avoid it, yet the giant's footwork was incredible, and he was on Buddha before he could fully recover.

The axe came in the uppercut maneuver once more, this time hitting its mark. The force of the blow sent Buddha onto his back, and Grool took full advantage of it. Grool heaved his great axe above his head and brought it downward. Buddha used the flat side of his blade to block the attack. Like a madman, Grool tried again with more strength, but Buddha had rolled away and got back to his feet.

Buddha pointed his blade toward the giant.

"Is this how you're going to protect your home? Swinging your axe around like it's your prick. You'd rather sleep in the woods, fuck your sister, and eat the shit of wild beasts than train properly with weapons?"

Grool the Giant grew irate at the insults. "You ignorant shit. We are free souls who would rather die than give up our will to live the way we choose."

"Souls?" Buddha laughed, looking around at Grool's men holding spears. "All I see are heathens."

The giant roared and charged him. Buddha charged and swung a series of strikes only to have them parried. Grool, with skill, operated his axe like it was another arm and kept Buddha at bay. However, Grool misjudged one swing, and Buddha sliced his chest, a nonlethal blow. Buddha pressed on, and the clashing of weapons continued. Buddha had fought many duels, many battles, but none ever compared to the skill or matched the strength of Grool the Giant.

Buddha and Grool were locked in, both weapons in a bind. Grool used his physique to his advantage, weighing himself down on Buddha. Grool performed a unique maneuver with his axe and disarmed Buddha. Before Buddha could fathom what just happened, he was rewarded with a punch from the giant, Buddha's helmet absorbing the blow. But the force made Buddha stagger backward, and Grool used the butt of his axe and quickly landed a blow to Buddha's face, his helmet absorbing the attack.

Buddha misjudged the giant's ability. Grool delivered a front kick to his abdomen, sending Buddha reeling backward, and the giant went on the offense. Rolling to his feet, Buddha recovered himself and was greeted with vicious attacks. Grool landed a strike so hard across the side of Buddha's helmet that the nanotechnology couldn't withstand it, and the helmet shattered. Buddha had fallen to the ground, yet he was thankful that his helmet took much of the force; nonetheless, his head was still concussed, and he was bleeding.

"This is your Lord of War? A lord who can't even hold onto his sword?" Grool said to the royal military. "What is that?" Grool put his hand to his ear to hear. "The great Buddha Bane has no words? Did I injure his pride with that little love tap?"

"No, Grool. You were outclassed with me having it, so I lost my sword so it could be a fair fight," Buddha responded.

Both fighters were exhausted, their breathing became heavy, and they began to feel their wounds. Grool charged Buddha. He brought his axe downward, and Buddha managed to grab the axe. Grool easily tossed him to the ground and kicked Buddha in his head, temporarily knocking him out. He grabbed a handful of Buddha's hair in his huge hands and lifted him up. Buddha, slowly regaining his senses, was weak and could barely walk as Grool paraded him around for all to see.

"Look and behold your commander. I treat him like I treat my wife." Grool paraded around in a circle. "Like a disobedient mate, I will beat you into submission."

Grool roughly shoved Buddha to the ground and stepped on Buddha's head, shifting his weight to apply more pressure. Buddha felt like his head was about to pop; death was creeping up on him.

Buddha's nano steel armor on his arms began to disintegrate and formed short blades that ran past his hands. Buddha stabbed the giant's leg. He heard the giant roar in pain as he staggered backward.

Buddha cursed himself for underestimating the giant; nonetheless, he charged him. Grool, hobbling on one leg while the other bled out, struggled to stay on the defensive. Buddha used his short blades to cut =his chest and stomach; Grool fell to one knee, bleeding and tired.

"It is done, Grool."

Buddha respected that he wanted a warrior's death and allowed Grool to recover himself a little more.

"I don't know if it is an honor or a damn tragedy to be bested by you, Buddha Bane." Grool tried speaking through heavy breaths.

"You might want to go with honor, preferably blessed." Buddha taunted in Grool in his final moments. Buddha punched his short blade into the giant's throat, and blood gushed as he retracted the blade.

―――――・―――――

Present Day

The room was eerily quiet. The only sounds were Augustus's slow heartbeat on the pulse oximeter. He lay in bed at a hospice, Tia beside him, an emotional wreck. She knew her father was bound for the afterlife, and even though she hated him, she still loved him. The room was well decorated, the walls coral, pictures of Miles and Tia when they were kids hung around. Even a photo of her mother smiling on their wedding day was present. Augustus enjoyed the finer things in life, like high-quality suits and top-tier furniture. His carpet was perfectly clean; they were shampooed twice a week. His curtains were fashionable because it had to be to complement the window that had an extraordinary view.

Tia looked at her father. He had lost so much weight that even she could pick him up and carry him. His mouth hung open, his teeth missing.

I did everything for you, even now I wipe your fucking ass. I am here with you at the end, and you still refuse to give me the one thing I want, Tia thought.

A woman appeared out of nowhere. Tia was completely oblivious to her as she stood over Augustus.

"Oh, Buddha," she said as she caressed his face.

Augustus opened his eyes, her voice always giving him new life. He looked at her. The woman was ugly beyond comparison—her skin gray, most of her hair absent, her eyes yellow and sad, her nose completely gone, her lips black, and her teeth rotten.

"Beautiful," Augustus managed to whisper out. Her looks meant nothing to him. His heart was set on her no matter her image. It still brought him pain to see her so beaten down. It only proved that he spent his time here failing her.

Tia looked up because her father managed to actually say something. She put her ear to his mouth, hoping that he was able to get another word out.

Please, fucking please, I am begging you. Just please. I worked so fucking hard, Daddy.

"Oh, my love," the woman said, smiling her horrible smile at his compliment. She went in closer to him. "Miles made the deal. I brought him back, but it took a lot of my strength to do so. Holding him here in this realm, along with you, will destroy me."

Augustus nodded, understanding what she was trying to tell him.

"Who are you talking to, Daddy? You talking to Momma? Uncle Troy?" Tia asked as she grasped her father's hand and kissed it.

"I searched all the past and the future, and no one would have done what you did for me. I will always be eternally grateful," the woman said. Her tears came as blood down her cheeks.

Augustus looked at her, his vision perfect for only a few more seconds.

"Name."

"It's Tia, Daddy!" Tia yelled. "I am right here. I have always been right here. Fucking acknowledge me!"

The woman bent down, kissed Augustus passionately on the lips, and whispered her name into his ear. The pleasure of her voice, the pleasure in her name, the power behind it no man could hear, it would only kill them. Augustus's eyes widened, his chest heaved. He smiled, feeling the best he had ever felt in his entire life. He saw worlds that couldn't be fathomed. He saw creatures bigger than buildings. He saw the past. He saw the future. He saw the sun and the moon, then the universe. He saw his son, then darkness; he was gone.

Tia watched him as he drew his last breath. She cried and kissed his forehead. She looked up and noticed the hospice nurse looking at her with shock. Tia was slightly embarrassed to have behaved like that in front of a stranger.

"You mention what you just saw to anyone, I swear I will end your fucking bloodline. Do you understand me?" Tia's tone was evil.

"Yes, yes, of course. Not a word," the nurse said.

Tia walked over to the nurse, a small woman in her twenties, and invaded her personal space, looking at her with all seriousness.

"My father is dead, and I just inherited one of the wealthiest organizations in the world. When you fucking talk to me, you put a fucking ma'am at the end of it."

The nurse's heart raced as if it were about to burst. She had never been so scared in her life; she was so frozen that she was almost speechless.

"Yes, yes, ma'am," the nurse responded.

"Do what you have to do. I want him taken care of as if he is God."

"Yes, ma'am," the nurse said, unable to look Tia in the eyes.

Tia walked past the nurse and out of the room. She heard the nurse sobbing recklessly, and it pleased her.

Scan QR Code to listen.
Expectations
by
M.U.R.K Entertainment

PART TWO

11

The day was blessed with blue sky, and the sun was beaming down on a perfect afternoon weather. Folks were dressed in their finest ebony attire, yet no one cared to boast about their threads. It wasn't often that family came together, and when they did, it was best to cherish those moments so you didn't end up like Ezekiel.

Ezekiel stood there in his finest ebony attire, looking up into the blue sky, with the sun shining on his face, praying for rain so it could mask his tears. Tears that he couldn't hold back, for how could he? How could he control these feelings that he had—this anger, sadness, and loneliness? The emotions were hitting him all at once, and just like getting punched in the stomach, it brought him to his knees. How could anyone hold these emotions back when they were burying the only family he had left, and the only person he could call little brother?

Ezekiel stayed to see the burial completed as he sat in the white chairs, his eyes fixed on the dirt poured on his brother's pearl white coffin. Some folks stayed, still weeping over his brother's passing, while others left, leaving him with pats on the shoulder and words such as "Sorry for your loss." He hated them. He hated them all—the folks still weeping, the folks who gave eulogies, and the fucks who told him sorry for his loss. Ezekiel hated the Loud 20s. He watched as they poured their liquors onto the ground. In his youth, he was a part of the infamous gang, and as much as he tried to keep his brother far from his exploits, it was a fiasco.

Vince sat in a chair next to Ezekiel. He was Ezekiel's close friend, and he was always down to do whatever needed to be done, no matter how dirty. They had known each other since boot camp, training to be a proud serving military member of the Districts. Ezekiel's violent tendencies caused him to be court-martialed, ending his tenure in the military. They conducted a methodical test that explored the deep root of his physiological makeup. It was found that Ezekiel was too brutal for the military, and he was labeled a danger to himself and other service members.

But those who were looking for men who could consciously do things that were labeled "immoral" were always in high demand. Ezekiel's skill set and his reputation sparked Tia Graves's interest. She advocated for him to join a team that she financed—a team that would make Bloody Hands no longer necessary. Ezekiel recommended Vince to be elected for the team, and over the last few years, they had been together despite other members dying in the field. Most never even made it off the table, trying to receive the Nano-Hive.

The team was small, and Ezekiel was successful in surviving the Nano-Hive implant and signaling the beacon, giving him a Flex. For the last six years, this confidential team had participated in the most perilous of operations—from massacres of affluent world leaders to destruction of chemical facilities, to complete annihilation of small villages or towns, and even to wiping out rogue forces off the face of the planet. Overall, they were a true force whose reputation contended with Bloody Hands. Their last mission was gathering a group of radicals and weaponizing them, training them to fight guerrilla warfare and instructing them on their invasion of Kurtaz.

Vince was tall and lanky, with pale skin and a slicked-back hairstyle that went well with his blond hair. He had little facial hair, but his trademark weaselly eyes were always scheming. Always. He, too, was in his finest ebony attire, paying his respects to the departed.

"Sorry about your loss, brother," Vince said.

Ezekiel said nothing, he just stared, fixated on the damn dirt.

"So, check this," Vince leaned close to Ezekiel, "I got word on who we might be looking for."

"And?" Ezekiel asked, his eyes still focused on the dirt.

"A few of the Loud 20s said they knew who was responsible. They gave names and descriptions."

"Who are they?"

Vince shrugged his shoulders. "Some fucks called Miles and Rikii. Zena is running their names now through the network. She has every Loud 20s member who can confirm their description in a room, looking at every Miles and Rikii in the Districts."

Ezekiel did not recognize the names. He already knew he was going to set the district on fire, but as for right now, this remaining time was for him and Jared. Vince saw Ezekiel's mood and thought it best to leave him with his younger brother.

"For blood," Vince said as he patted Ezekiel's shoulder and took his leave.

"For blood," Ezekiel responded, but his voice was a whisper.

———•—•———

Miles opened his eyes and realized he was still in a hospital bed. He looked over to see Rikii, dressed in a gray sweatshirt and pants, sleeping in the hospital recliner seat. Miles smiled at her, all bundled up in the sheets. He always enjoyed watching her sleep peacefully. His attention was quickly redirected to the TV that was on, and because he could no longer sleep and didn't want to wake Rikii, he indulged in the news.

"Talking about miracles, just months ago all evidence pointed to Kurtaz falling. The country that has been a superpower was somehow dwarfed by an unknown enemy, officially named the Invaders. Journalists reported cities being overrun. We had video footage of the destruction in Rasheeda. There had been reports of citizens of Kurtaz fleeing to other countries, and the Kurtazian government being at odds over military maneuvers. Their end was transparent, but weeks ago, the sovereign supreme of Kurtaz clearly stated that he and his government agreed that they would not bend a knee. Well, as of today, that perseverance is paying off. Reports are coming in that the Invaders force has weakened, and the Kurtazian military took full advantage of this. It has been a bloodbath thus far, and the war is far from over. But we can say now, no one knows what the outcome will be.

"Moving on to other news, today marks two weeks since the shooting at Roxy's, a popular nightclub in New Area. We'd like to offer our condolences, once again, to the families of those who lost their lives in the tragic event. Also, there has been an update on Augustus Graves Jr., a survivor of that horrific night. It has been said his injuries might have been severe, but due to the competence of the district's best doctors, he is making remarkable recovery. It would have been a true tragedy to lose both Augustus Graves Sr. and Jr."

Miles smiled at the comment. *That's what a billion coins gets ya.* He almost forgot how quickly his body could heal from such wounds, it had been a long time since he was in such a condition. Miles was amused at the photo of himself that the news channel displayed on television. It was a good gambit by Styles to always use an outdated photo of Miles not looking his best, keeping up the act that he has been in and out of rehab for drug addiction. And there was also the added benefit that such an old, low-quality photo would make it hard for people to recognize what he looked like now. Miles showed no emotion upon hearing of the passing of his father. All that meant was he and Rikii could be free, and to him, that was the best news.

"Oh, I would totally fuck him," Rikii said, looking at Miles's old photo on the TV.

"Hey, beautiful," Miles responded as his eyes followed Rikii, making her way from under the covers of the recliner to his side to kiss him. "How long was I out this time?"

"Let's see..." Rikii pretended to think "Last time we spoke, it was two days ago."

"Damn."

"Mm-hmm."

"Well, good news is I feel a lot better."

Rikii lifted Miles's sheets and his hospital gown to look at his wound, which was a scar now. Even the hospital staff was amazed by how such a recovery happened. Rikii spent the last two weeks fighting off female nurses who came in and out of Miles's room to get a peek at him. His healing wasn't the only thing remarkable, but when he got X-rays and his birth information was inputted in the system, people didn't understand how a forty-seven-year-old man looked thirty, with a body still in its prime.

Rikii couldn't help but notice Miles's morning erection and decided to fondle him.

Miles let out a long pleasurable moan.

"Hurry and get me out of this hospital, and I will drain you of every drop," Rikii whispered into Miles ear as she continued to stroke him.

There was a knock at the door.

12

Miles looked up, and to his surprise, it was someone he did not expect—Tia. She came dressed for business in a black suit that fit her well. Her beauty couldn't be ignored, but Tia never relied on her looks. She used her intellect and wit.

"The fuck are you doing here?" Miles asked.

"I can't come and check up on my brother?" Tia's tone was not caring. "Plus, someone had to do damage control for you." Tia made her way to Miles's bedside. "How are you feeling, seriously?"

"I will be out of here soon. I feel a lot better," Miles admitted.

"I have to tell you about Daddy," Tia said, with no emotion in her voice.

Miles was quiet. He knew his father was horribly sick, and after hearing the news, he knew his father was dead.

"Did you hear me?" Tia asked.

"I did," Miles responded, but his attention was on the television, which he flickered through, landing on reality TV, his mind elsewhere.

"You wanna talk about it?" Tia asked.

"Talk to you? About Dad?" Miles laughed. "I'd rather eat a grenade."

"Good. Hurry up and heal because we need you back at work."

Miles and Rikii gave each other a quick quizzical look. "What do you mean back at work? We are done, Tia."

Tia looked at Rikii, who didn't make eye contact with her, and then at Miles.

"What do you mean we are done?"

"This was the last job," Miles said, with a tone in his voice.

"A job in New Area?" Tia paused for a moment. "You're telling me that's why y'all were here in New Area? And I thought you two were just fucking off, deliberately ignoring my calls."

"Wait a minute," Miles sat himself up in the bed. "Styles said—"

Tia cut Miles off with a hand gesture. "I understand now. This must have been Daddy's call."

Daddy must've found out what I was up to. In any case, Miles can fuck off. Rikii leaving, it will never happen, Tia thought.

"Listen, Miles, Daddy is dead, and it seems that he may have wanted you to enjoy the rest of your life in peace, and I am going to honor that."

"Like I give a fuck if you honor it or not. We were promised coin, new identities, and not to be disturbed ever again," Miles informed Tia, who didn't seem to be listening to him but instead was focused on Rikii.

"You are so fucking gorgeous it makes me just want to do things." Tia ran her fingers through Rikii's finger waves, giving her a lusty look.

Miles noticed how uncomfortable Rikii was becoming.

"That's enough," Miles's tone very blunt.

"I will give you the benefit of the doubt," Tia said, running her fingers along Rikii's lips. "You deserve to hang it all up. But Rikii here doesn't even have a decade of experience and is still in her prime. Plus, she needs to come home. She has responsibilities she has been ignoring."

"I said we are done!" Miles stated again, firmly.

"And I said you are done!" Tia said, backing off from Rikii, her full attention on Miles now. "She doesn't belong to you. She is the property of the Graves Foundation. And last time I checked, I run the fucking foundation, so she is my property."

"If running the foundation makes your pussy wet, then so be it, sis, but Rikii ain't going with you," Miles said.

Tia smiled. "Why do I even give you energy, Miles? Enjoy retirement." she said. "Rikii, get your things. We are leaving."

Rikii was stuck. She couldn't make eye contact with Miles or Tia. She was just frozen.

"I get it, girl. You love him. But this is why we don't fall in love, because it affects our job performance. Trust me, I would know," Tia said as she pulled out her PDP. Tia fingered it for a moment and smiled. "Last time, Rikii. Let's go."

Miles reached out and took Rikii's hand. "Hey, you do what you want to do. You want to go with her, then go. I won't be mad at you. You want to stay with me, then stay."

Tia grew impatient. "OK, Rikii, if that's how it's going to be, then fine. I wish you all the best. Oh, and there is this." Tia handed Miles a thumb drive. "Seems Daddy had some last words for you."

"Did you get one?" Miles asked as he took the drive.

Tia smiled, but Miles saw the sadness in her eyes. "No. No, I didn't."

Back in the Day

The punches came, and Jared felt every blow as he lay there, taking his beating from the neighborhood bully. The other teenage bystanders cheered and roared as the two teenagers tussled on the ground. Jared did well for the first twenty seconds before he was taken to the ground and easily overpowered by his opponent. Jared always hated being the runt among his peers. It disqualified him from certain activities, especially with the girls, and it made getting his ass kicked extremely easy.

Lenny, a sophomore in high school who was built like he had already graduated from a university, showed no mercy on Jared. For Lenny, beating the shit out of other people increased his popularity, which in turn made the girls wet after him. He noticed Jared hanging with his friends, and out of nowhere, he grabbed Jared and tossed him to the ground. Jared stood and fought like his older brother taught him, but his size kept him from any possible success of winning a fight.

Jared lay there helplessly, taking the hits, and knew his face was gonna swell, and he was going to hear it from his brother again, who only gets mad at him because his mom would yell at him for not watching Jared. The crowd of roaring bystanders hushed suddenly, and Lenny, so engulfed in delivering his ass whooping on Jared, didn't realize his recompense was right behind him.

Ezekiel, twenty-two with a no-fucks-given attitude, grabbed Lenny and tossed him off Jared. Ezekiel's face went evil when he saw his brother bleeding and crying. With a nod, he ordered his entourage, the Loud 20s, to help Jared up.

"You want some too, bitch?" Lenny, in his arrogance, said before he could assess who he was talking to. He sized Ezekiel up and instantly regretted his words. Ezekiel stood, in a sleeveless cutoff denim vest, his arms showing that he was very apt when it came to athletics, his vest matching his denim jeans and all-white sneakers, and his yellow-and-blue bandannas hanging from his back pockets.

"Aye, Zeke, I ain't know this was your peoples," Lenny said, looking for some mercy; he wasn't granted any.

Ezekiel took his firearm from his waistband, and with quickness, he hit Lenny hard with it. Lenny went down, and Ezekiel got on top of him. He beat Lenny with his firearm until Lenny's face was bloody.

"You come near my brother again, I'm gonna rape your lil sister while my boys run a train on yo momma, then I will kill all of you. You get me?" Ezekiel's words were not to be taken lightly. Everyone on the west end knew Ezekiel was one of the Loud 20s triggermen.

Lenny, who just lost a few teeth, nodded, indicating that he understood.

Ezekiel was not satisfied and continued to beat Lenny to an inch of his life. Ezekiel looked up, and those bystanders who were roaring and cheering Jared getting his ass kicked were no longer present.

"Just a black eye and busted lip, you be OK," Ezekiel said as he assessed his brother's wounds.

"I almost had him," Jared said.

"Yeah, OK, but look, you ain't gotta worry about him no more, bro."

"Yeah, but you gotta worry about Mom."

Ezekiel laughed. "Fuck, yeah. She mos def gonna beat my ass when she sees your face."

———•·•———

Present Day

"I was told I could find you here," Tia said.

Ezekiel woke from his slight nap down memory lane. The funeral was long over, and Jared was fully buried, but Ezekiel couldn't bring himself to leave. He was too ashamed that he wasn't there when Jared needed him the most.

"You want to cry all day, or you want some get back?" Tia asked. Ezekiel looked up and saw Tia Graves, who looked spectacular. He was grateful that she gave him the opportunity to join her team of misfits, but today he was just not in the mood for her shit.

"The fuck you talking about?" he asked.

"Check your PDP. I sent you the details already."

Ezekiel looked at his PDP, touched it, and in holographic mode, opened a manila folder. He skimmed some of the contents, and his eyes widened. A photo of Augustus Miles Graves Jr. showed up, doing a 360 rotation in hologram mode. Under the head was confidential information that not even Ezekiel could believe.

Ezekiel scrolled through the contents, reviewing old hit lists that were marked completed. He reviewed old photos of dead bodies, burned buildings, and articles of assassinations and suicides.

"Are you telling me that your brother, the junkie, did all this?" Ezekiel asked.

Ezekiel looked at the file again. "Contracts like these live up to reputation of Bloody Hands."

Tia gave Ezekiel a look that confirmed his statement.

"Ain't no fucking way," Ezekiel whispered to himself.

"He was the prototype, but my father fell in love with his abilities and weaponized him," Tia said, validating Ezekiel's newfound revelation.

"Damn. Well, at least he had a Daddy, but what does this gotta do with me?"

"Have you seen the news? The picture of my brother was up there."

"Yeah, said he received life-threatening injuries. But the news said he was gonna pull through."

Tia paused, not sure how her next comment was going to go, but it was better to just rip off the Band-Aid. "He was at the club to kill all the barons."

It took a few moments for everything to register for Ezekiel. He had been under so much stress the past week, and with little sleep, he found it hard to process some information. But once the information was fully registered in his mind, he began to connect the dots.

Miles and Rikii.

Augustus Miles Graves.

Bloody Hands.

Ezekiel turned his head slowly toward Tia.

"What are you telling me? Are you telling me that it was you who gave the kill order?"

"No, but since I inherited everything I am the Graves Foundation, so in a way, yes. But I didn't have knowledge that your little brother was running shit down here."

"He wasn't running shit. He was a soft fuck who could only follow, so how he made it to boss status is one hell of an unsolved mystery."

"I get your frustration, but let me make it up to you. An eye for an eye." Tia signaled to Ezekiel's PDP. "Kill my brother, but the woman he's with, you will return to me unharmed. This won't be easy. You will lose most of your team doing this, so be prepared for that."

"Like I give a fuck. They knew what they were signing up for. How do you want this done? You want it quiet?"

"Do it based on how you feel as long as it's done ASAP," Tia said as she turned to take her leave.

Scorched earth it is, Ezekiel thought. "How do I find him?"

"I placed a tracker on him. The details are in the file I sent. I'd hurry if I were you."

13

Rikii stood in the shower. allowing the water to rinse the soap off her naked body; Miles came and joined in behind her. No words were said between them. Words were a second language to them, and they communicated in another form. Miles wrapped his arms around Rikii and felt her relax a bit. Rikii ran her hands along his arms. She took his left in her left hand, their rings complementing one another. Miles bent down gently and kissed the right side of her neck as he caressed her small breasts. He kept his eyes open, studying Rikii's privates, watching it slowly grow with every kiss until it became fully erect.

Miles reached down, grabbed Rikii's privates, and stroked it as he kissed Rikii on the side of her face; every kiss was slow and drawn out. Miles became more passionate as he massaged Rikii's throat, forcing her to turn her head so he could insert his tongue into her mouth. Her body squirmed from his tongue and hands. Rikii kept her mouth near Miles's nostrils, for she wanted to breathe her soul into him. Miles felt Rikii about to climax and stilled his hand; Rikii had surrendered herself years ago to Miles, her privates and her climax belonged to him. Miles placed Rikii's hands on the wall, then gripped her buttocks and gently massaged her crevices. He leaned into her, allowing her to feel his hardness; he slowly inserted himself into her.

Miles relished Rikii's loud moan and held himself inside her, allowing Rikii to rock back and forth on him. Rikii knew not to stop until Miles started thrusting back, and he let Rikii work, Miles in awe of the water trickling off Rikii's backside. Miles gave one powerful thrust, making Rikii grunt. He enjoyed her grunting and gave her a few powerful thrusts before slowing down to how Rikii preferred it—slow all the way out and slow all the way back in. Miles picked up the pace; her beautiful legs trying to run.

Miles loved her more than he could put into words. Every thrust was with passion; every stroke of Rikii's privates was a message that said I can't live without you. Rikii was moaning loudly. Miles took her off the wall, and Rikii started to stroke her own privates, her well-manicured foot spasmodic. He removed her hand, and Rikii turned to look at Miles, her eyes begging him to let her climax.

Miles gave her a look that told her when he was good and ready, he would let her finish. He pulled out of her, turned her around, wrapped his hands around her throat, and kissed her. He tightly grabbed her buttocks and lifted her; Rikii wrapped her legs around him. Miles turned off the shower. He carried Rikii, who was smothering his face with kisses, to their hotel bedroom. He threw Rikii on the bed, and she lay on her back, legs spread, her privates eager.

Miles looked at her, her hazel eyes locked on his lips. She bit her bottom lip in anticipation. Miles grabbed and fondled her scrotum, and Miles watched her eyes roll back. He took her into his mouth and felt her body spasm as she let out a curse; Miles watched her toes curl. He continued to possess her, and the only thought that passed through his mind was he knew he would end civilizations for her. He flipped her onto her stomach and positioned himself to lick her crevices, making her moan uncontrollably. Miles mounted her and inserted himself once more. He slid in as deep as he could go, wrapping his arms around Rikii's neck.

Rikii kept her legs up and moaned loud, but Miles cut off the moan by kissing her. He continued to make love to her, feeling her body spasm from pleasure, slow all the way out and slow all the way back in. Miles pulled out of Rikii and lay down, both covered in sweat. Rikii gathered herself, then stood on the bed and stood over Miles, who admired her body. He watched her squat and insert his manhood into her. She didn't break eye contact as she bounced on him.. Miles spat into his hand and began stroking Rikii's privates, slowing her bouncing down as she was trapped within Miles's hand, and she refused to tell him to stop.

She gave him the pleading eyes once more as her mouth hung open. She rubbed her breast and stomach, and Miles knew she couldn't hold it much longer. Miles continued to stroke her, not giving her permission to give in. Rikii couldn't hold it in anymore.

"Baby, I can't hold it. I can't hold it. Fuck, I can't—" Rikii let out a massive moan mixed with a grunt and her body vibrated as she finished hard all over Miles's chest. He kept stroking her through her climax. Rikii fell onto the bed, exhausted, her chest heaving, her hazel eyes peering into Miles's soul.

They lay there looking at each other. What words existed to describe how they felt? Their bodies, their minds, and their souls were one.

"Let me ask you something," Miles said.

"Baby, after that climax, you can ask me anything," Rikii replied.

"It's been bothering me. What did my sister mean the other day when she said you have responsibilities? And why was she touching you like that?"

Rikii went pale.

"You can talk to me. You know that. I just want to protect you. That's all," Miles said as he caressed Rikii's face.

"I know, but let me go get a towel so I can clean you up. I kinda made a mess," Rikii said as she got up and went into the bathroom. Rikii came back with the towel and began wiping Miles's chest.

"Have you opened the thumb drive yet?" Rikii asked, hoping her efforts of moving the conversation off her would divert Miles's attention.

"I haven't. I was hoping you could watch it with me," Miles responded.

Rikii kissed Miles. "Of course."

They sat at the desk and turned on the built-in computer. Miles inserted the drive, waiting for the files to load. He could only think of the words he wanted to say to his father, if he was present at his deathbed. The words weren't going to be anything nice; he hated the man so much, his life wasted, only looked at as a weapon and not a son. They never had conversations about cinemas, sports, books, women, or anything that normal dads talk to their sons about. It was always what weapons he needed a critique on his job performance, or if there have been any discrepancies with the Nano-Secs. Miles was happy that Rikii, who rubbed his shoulders, was with him.

"I swear, if this man says 'I love you' in this video, I'm gonna throw this fucking desk out the window," Miles said.

It sparked a laugh out of Rikii. "Why is it taking so long to load?"

"Yeah, I don't know, babe. Maybe the system is just slow. It could be the hotel has a weak signal."

Miles fiddled with the screen some more, and a folder appeared.

"See, the system is just slow as shit," Miles said as he pressed the folder to open its contents.

"What the fuck?" Rikii said as she looked at the password encryption on the screen.

"Yeah, what the fuck? Tia didn't say jack shit about a password."

He sat puzzled and wondered why Tia would give him a blank drive. Miles looked at Rikii, hoping she could summon a conclusion. *That fucking bitch*, Miles thought.

"Well, how about we get something to eat while you think about cracking the code?" Rikii suggested.

"Room service?"

"Nah, no one wants that, boring as shit," Rikii responded.

———— • ————

"We have lost our way. It seems that we were so used to peace that when opposition came, we forgot ourselves," Omar said, letting his words sink in. Omar was a slender man, his skin darkly tanned, his thick black curly hair present, and his beard long and well-conditioned. He dressed in ivory linen, customary for people in this part of the world where the weather knew its mind.

Styles, dressed in fine clothing, sat and listened to Omar rant. They sat on the balcony of Omar's home, drinking coffee and eating biscuits. Omar, son of a prominent Kurtazian military general, earned his status quo through business management. He later turned to politics, his true calling. Styles had to admit to himself that the view from Omar's balcony was gorgeous. He could see the waters in the distance, and the lack of corporate buildings and skyscrapers was relaxing.

"For decades we wanted to desperately become a world power once more, but these old fools thought that Kurtaz's glory days were enough to strike fear into other nations, and look at what happened. A group of savages with no aim or purpose has their boots on our necks. Honestly it's like fighting wild beasts. Only they know what they want, and we assume that they are just hungry."

"And again, what did you want to do about it?" Styles asked.

"The old ways are not working. They never did. This country needs reform. It needs structure. It needs individuals willing to put the work in."

"Well, you're not going to be able to do any of that if this war continues." Styles sipped his coffee and indulged in a complimentary biscuit. "What Tia proposes—"

"What Tia proposes is treason," Omar interrupted.

"She proposes a door that once you open and walk through, you are walking into power."

"Fuck you. What power? I will be in debt, which means she will rule over me."

"We all answer to someone, Omar."

"Would you take this deal?" Omar asked with intent to measure Styles's character.

Styles, nobody's fool, saw the play that Omar was making and decided to make his own gambit.

"Tia is ambitious. She will gain her rightful place in politics. That is for sure, but me personally, I have no interest in such things. So, to answer your question, no, I wouldn't take the deal. The deal that I will take, if I was you, will be the one that I propose to you."

Omar looked at Styles and observed that he was serious in his disposition.

"You have my attention."

"What I said was true. You take Tia's deal, and you walk into power, but if you take my deal..." Styles reached into his pocket and pulled out a blank black card, handing it to Omar. "You will walk into immortality."

Omar reached and took the card from Styles. Upon grabbing it, the blank card illuminated with gold lettering that spelled out Ryse.

"I heard about this secret cult back when I was studying at the university in the Districts. They've been around for years. I have no interest in such nonsense."

"Do I come across as a man who deals with nonsense?" Styles asked as he sipped his coffee.

———— · ————

Tia's PDP rang as she sat in her stretch transport, enjoying her glass of wine.

"What is it?"

"The deal with Omar is done," Styles said.

The news was enough to make Tia pause mid-sip.

"We secured Kurtaz?" Tia was ready to cuss Styles out, for she hadn't heard from him in days.

"Yes. He agreed to the five-year contract, that you would supply his military with firearms and advocate on his behalf to overthrow the current regime."

It all came to a head; Tia had planned it perfectly. The Ryse wanted the lands in Rae so badly they agreed to the conditions to sell it once her daddy died. The plan was simple: have the Ryse finance a group of radicals to invade Kurtaz, keeping her fingerprints clear. Tia had sent her own team in to help facilitate the training of the radicals, which proved useful.

She knew Omar back from their university days, when he studied abroad. He loved to talk about what he would do in the Kurtazian government after he graduated. The thing about Omar was he didn't have a push to take charge. So the idea of becoming general of the Districts came to fruition for Tia. She knew she needed to have all of Kurtaz under her heel, not just a few acres of land. But Augustus Sr., in his wisdom and experience, saw what Tia was doing, and as for one more fuck you, he sent Bloody Hands to cut the operation, but he was too late.

Kurtaz had seen the writing on the wall and knew that without the help of the Graves Foundation, the Invaders would have been successful. Having the Kurtazian government under her thumb meant her authority in the Districts was above the presidency. With her reach crossing all the way to the Free Territories, Southern Isles, and backdoor deals with the districts' government, she could advocate for herself for presidency. But she needed to first earn the title of general, then be groomed for president. Her father never liked politics. He did business with whomever had coin to spend, but Tia had bigger dreams.

"Styles, I need you on a flight back immediately. I need you to set up a meeting with President Floyd so we can properly explain why making me his second-in-command will behoove him for his next term."

"Yeah, I got you. One more thing, did you tell Miles?"

"Well about that..."

"Cousin, what the fuck did you do?" Styles asked.

Styles had always been loyal to the foundation. His father helped build it before his mysterious death. Styles had also always been eager to please Augustus Sr., who shared the same face as Styles's father. Growing up he would look out for Tia; he was very acute when it came to Tia's coldness and how it would land her in trouble. They became more like siblings than cousins when Miles was sent to the field and her mother, Latoya, killed herself.

"I sent a team to kill him and to retrieve Rikii," Tia responded.

"Are you fucking insane? Why not just let the homie fucking retire? He isn't going to say shit. And you taking Rikii is going to make shit worse. You know how Miles is when it comes to her. Your obsession with her needs to fucking stop. You can carry on without her.

You are so fucking close to running the Districts. I don't understand why you are insistent on fucking it all up."

"When the fuck were you going to tell me you were going behind my back to make a deal with Daddy?"

Styles remained quiet.

"Exactly. I thought you were on my side, cousin," Tia said.

"It was his final wish. How the hell can I tell him no after all he did for me?"

"Shit, the way you kissed his ass growing up, any man with that much tongue in his ass would have put you through law school." Tia laughed, the wine finally kicking in.

"The fuck, Tia?"

Tia was hurt. She couldn't understand why Rikii chose Miles over her. She never took rejection really well. She thought she was used to it by now—Dad ignored her, and Mom was too drugged out of her mind to even realize she had a daughter.

"I got it handled," Tia said.

"He's going to kill all of us if you go through with this. Your team of degenerates won't get the job done."

Tia hung up. She was irritated at the truth of what Styles said. But she couldn't let Rikii go. She would risk the presidency for that. And as for Miles, she couldn't stomach the thought of him always being a threat to her ambitions; he had to go.

Her phone rang again, and she saw the number was of her nanny.

"Yes, Maria," Tia said.

"Good evening, Ms. Graves. I'm calling because Zheff has been asking to speak to you," Maria said as she shifted the screen to face a little boy, no older than nine years of age.

He was a handsome little boy with a tan complexion and four years of dreadlocks coming down his face. He smiled, his front teeth missing.

"Hey, Momma," Zheff said.

"Hey, look, Mom is still on business, but I will be home by tomorrow OK?" Tia said, trying to end the conversation quickly.

"All right, see you tomorrow. Love you," Zheff replied.

"I love you too," Tia said as she hung up.

Tia reached into her purse and pulled out a small bottle that contained a clear liquid. The bottle contained an eyedropper, which she used to disperse a drop in each of her eyes. She felt high and stretched herself out and faded.

14

People, in a rush to get to nowhere, were busy tonight. The streets were decorated with transports honking, music blasting, while people were sitting in traffic. They rushed across crosswalks and occupying the sidewalks. The only ones benefiting from the busy night were the small bodegas selling their concessions.

"How the hell are you still hungry?" Miles held the door of the bodega open while Rikii stepped out, stuffing her mouth with a sausage link.

"All those extracurricular activities you put me through builds up an appetite," Rikii spoke with her mouth full.

"Lord, Rikii, you don't have no chill, do you?" Miles walked alongside Rikii to the side of the bodega.

"You sure there ain't anything you want to do before we leave the Districts?" Miles asked.

"Yeah, baby, I'm good. I know you want to get out of here quickly."

Rikii took a step in front of Miles, eating her sausage link; she sized him up. Miles was dressed in black boots, black jeans, a long-sleeved olive-green button-down with most of the buttons undone at the top, revealing his chest and expensive gold chain. It complemented his expensive stud earrings. He was well groomed, donning his typical hairstyle—two long braids going to his shoulder blades with the sides of his head shaved. His beard was trimmed low, as he feared the gray hairs that remained persevering.

"You look fine as fuck, baby." Rikii gave Miles a lusty look.

"Trying to keep up with you, my love," Miles said as he sized Rikii up. She wore her black-heeled boots and olive-green cargo pants with a long-sleeved black shirt tucked in. She was extremely gorgeous, her makeup well done, even though it wasn't needed, and her pixie haircut with finger waves was just as vibrant.

Miles adored her. He knew once they left the Districts, he was going to take Rikii far away and drown her in his love for the rest of his days.

A transport, whose headlights ruined Miles and Rikii's moment, crept up on them. The lights shone bright, blinding both Miles and Rikii. Miles activated his Flex, looking through the bright lights.

"What the fuck?" Miles said aloud.

Miles heard the doors of the transport slide open and saw people coming out. Miles grabbed Rikii and ushered her back to the front of the bodega.

"Miles!" Rikii shouted.

Men dressed tactically pointed rapid firearms at them. Miles looked to run into the street, but another group of men dressed the same also had rapid firearms aimed at them. People ran frantically, and transports honked as the gunmen interrupted street traffic with their formation.

Fuck, they got us pinned, Miles thought.

"Release the woman," one of the men ordered Miles.

I wouldn't hand this woman over to God if he asked.

"Come get her," Miles said as he squeezed Rikii's elbow, giving her the signal. Rikii activated her Flex, ducked, and bear crawled out of the way to leave Bloody Hands to do what he did best.

"She's Flexing." A gunman called out.

How the fuck they know about Flex? Miles thought.

The gunmen open fired on Miles, their bullets ricocheting off him. The team in front of Miles closed in on him, and that was their mistake. Miles grabbed the firearm of one of the gunmen, disarming him quickly. He went to shoot the firearm, but the trigger was locked. It needed a DNA signature to release the trigger.

Military grade, Miles thought.

Miles twirled the weapon and swung it at the head of the gunman and took the opportunity to punch the gunman in the face. More shots rang out from the gunmen behind Miles, who saw the gunmen in the street being disarmed and killed by Rikii.

Satisfied that Rikii was secure and handling herself, he went to deal with the gunmen shooting at him from behind. Before he could close the distance, he was tackled into the glass windows of the bodega. Glass shattered everywhere as Miles and his opponent hit the floor inside the bodega.

Ezekiel stood above Miles, Flex activated. He grabbed Miles and threw him into the ceiling, shattering the lights. Miles hit the ground hard, and Ezekiel grabbed him and threw him hard into the coolers, drinks falling upon Miles.

"Get yo ass up, Bloody Hands," Ezekiel said.

Miles gathered himself, irate that he just got tossed like a child.

"What you want with Rikii?"

Ezekiel stood at five feet, ten inches, dressed in all-black tactical gear. His sleeveless shirt revealed his muscular and heavily tattooed arms. His bulletproof vest held multiple magazines, wrist restraints, and grenades. Ezekiel ignored Miles's question and swung a punch at Miles, who let it land.

The force and power of the punch took Miles off his feet, and Ezekiel rubbed his painful hand.

Miles rose and charged toward Ezekiel, swinging a series of punches and landing a couple of jabs, making his opponent bleed. Ezekiel grabbed Miles by the shirt and swung him back into the coolers, punching him repeatedly. Miles felt no pain, just force from the blows.

Damn, he strong as fuck.

Miles timed it right; he caught Ezekiel's fist and jammed his thumb into Ezekiel's eye, causing him to holler in pain and step back. Miles scooped Ezekiel by the legs, running him into the racks that held food and candies. They hit the floor, both getting up quickly to take the offensive. Miles was quicker and landed an uppercut to Ezekiel's face.

The blackout was quick, Ezekiel somehow maintained consciousness after the blow. Ezekiel pretended to be weak and wobbly, as he saw Miles coming toward him. Miles went to throw another punch, but Ezekiel grabbed Miles by the throat and slammed him hard into the ground. The floor cracked from Ezekiel's Flex of strength and Miles's Flex of invulnerability. Ezekiel stomped on Miles's head a few times before backing off to catch his breath.

Miles stood up.

"Yep, you smell like you have Tia's juices all over your face."

The hell she wants Rikii so badly for?

"Why did you kill Jared?" Ezekiel asked.

"Who?" Miles responded.

Gunshots rang out, and Miles's heart sank at the thought of Rikii fighting all the gunmen alone. But he remembered that they wanted him to release her, which indicated that they wanted her alive.

"Jared!" Ezekiel yelled, taking out the yellow-and-blue bandanna from his pocket and throwing it on the floor.

Oh, that Jared.

"Son, I don't give a fuck if I ripped your mother's head from her body and skull fucked her, you die either way," Miles answered.

Ezekiel smiled.

"See, that's what I like about you, and what I like even more is that woman you're with. See, I was ordered to make sure she was extracted without harm, but that bitch is as good as dead when I'm done with you."

"Fuck you still talking for then?" Miles asked as he assumed his fighting stance.

Ezekiel activated his Flex and ran toward Miles, who sidestepped him. Ezekiel tried to close the distance but received a kick to the gut for his efforts and fell to his knees. Miles came in to deliver a punch; Ezekiel exploded up, grabbing Miles and rushing him into the slushy machine. Red, blue, and brown slushy gushed everywhere. Miles tried to break the lock, but Ezekiel's strength was too great, and in his anger, he was feeling no pain.

He tossed Miles hard to the ground and quickly grabbed his handgun, pointing it at Miles.

Miles quickly punched Ezekiel in his privates and scrambled to get to his feet. Ezekiel persevered through the pain, removed his tranquilizer, and shot at Miles, who was running to the entrance of the bodega. Miles fell, his body spasmodic, as the bullet had hit him.

Ezekiel stood over Miles.

"You're probably wondering what the fuck just hit you." Ezekiel showed Miles the handgun that was clear enough to see the components on the inside and didn't look like a gun at all. "This bad boy is a specialized tranquilizer. I like to use this when one of my boys with a Flex gets out of control. It shuts their Flex down temporarily."

Ezekiel, his Flex activated, punched Miles repeatedly, blood gushing from his face. He reached into his vest, took out a hand grenade, and hooked it on Miles's pants.

For blood, Ezekiel thought.

"Hold this," Ezekiel said as he removed the pin from the grenade. Ezekiel quickly lifted Miles up, and with all his strength, he threw Miles into the back of the store.

15

"Get up, boy," Augustus Sr. said, with a disappointed tone.

Miles woke up and looked about his surroundings; he was covered in debris, black residue from the explosion, and random food and drink of the bodega. He looked up and saw his father dressed in one of his finest suits, but his face looked decades younger.

"Oh, fuck. No, not this shit again," Miles said as he removed the debris and tried standing up. "I hear you finally gave up the ghost."

"Seems like it."

"Thank God," Miles said. He walked to the entrance, past his father and over the mess of the store.

"Where are you going, boy?"

"I have to go get Rikii. Please go fuck off and burn in peace, will ya?"

"How about a little gratitude."

"The fuck you talking about?"

"Your Flex was inactive, and you ate a grenade, and you're still whole."

Miles paused because what his dead father just said was true, *How the hell did I survive that?*

"Apparently you dumbass made a deal, and you haven't made good on it yet. So right now, dying wouldn't be of benefit," Augustus Sr. said.

"Ah, I see. Well, tell my creditor I said thank you," Miles said as he took his leave, but he was instantly back in his old training room. The aroma of the mats, punching bags, training gloves, and weights all brought back memories that Miles had forgotten.

"You gotta be fucking kidding me."

Augustus Sr. looked at his son, and for the first time, he actually saw him. Miles's face was handsome but had a good mixture of his mother, Latoya, in him. For the first time, he saw his son not as a weapon but just as a man—a man who was in love.

I remember the feeling. All my past victories were because of love, but I found something that was greater than her. I just lost myself in the process, getting back what was lost, Augustus Sr. thought.

"So what are you going to do?" Augustus Sr. asked as he sat in his old chair, where he would watch a young Miles train relentlessly.

"Why the hell are you still here?"

Augustus Sr. shrugged. "Someone thought it would be best that my punishment was to spend my entirety with you."

"Sounds more like my fucking punishment."

"You never answered my question. I asked what you are going to do now?"

Miles was irritated. He had left Rikii, and now his dead father thought it best to annoy him in his desperate time.

"I'm going to send your daughter to you so you can have some company. Apparently, even in death, you want nothing to do with your wife. You just want to still play with your toys."

"OK, boy, listen—"

"Shut the fuck up!" Miles said. "I don't know why the hell you are here, or why you brought me to this place of misery. But I don't need you. I don't want you. You are nothing to me. I hope you burn for a thousand lifetimes, you pathetic fuck."

"You will be joining me when your time comes."

"At least I won't be no coward about it. I will take my sins and own them like a real fucking man."

"Lord, have mercy. You're a grown ass man, and you're still butt hurt. Grow a pair. I did what I did, oh fucking well. There is no use in crying over it. Unless you're going to pull a time machine out your ass, you need to move the fuck on, Miles."

"Wow, real good words of encouragement, Pops." Miles paced the mat room. "Let me ask you this. Were those the final words you had for me on the video?"

Augustus Sr. looked at Miles, bemused. "What video?"

Miles ceased his pacing and registered his father's answer. "That fucking bitch placed a tracker on me."

"Before I died, I realized that Tia made a deal with the Ryse to give them the lands in Rae. The Ryse by no means can obtain those lands. They are Shifters pulling strings from the shadows. That's why I sent you to New Area—"

"I don't care about your lands in Rae. I don't care about the fucking Ryse. I need to be sent back," Miles said.

"We need to stop the Ryse first, Miles. Rikii will be fine."

"You have to be the stupidest motherfucker if you think I care about some fucking lands or a fucking Shifter. Rikii is more important."

Augustus looked at his son quizzically, as if he had some sort of déjà vu regarding this conversation.

" If the Ryse succeed in their plans, then the world is doomed, and it's on your hands, Miles."

"You ain't name me Bloody Hands for no reason."

Miles looked up and saw that his father had vanished. He was happy to be back in the store, in reality. Miles looked out the store's shattered windows and saw the authorities on scene having a shoot-out with the men he encountered earlier. Miles cracked his knuckles and rolled his shoulders.

They say the road to hell is paved with good intentions. I say fuck that. I'm going to pave it with blood and bullets.

16

It was complete madness, but Rikii was able to remain calm in the fray. She was in the midst of fighting her abductors when the authorities showed up and started shooting. She managed to take cover behind a transport and watch her abductors erase the authorities from the face of the planet.

Their tact was immaculate, and the only thing Rikii could think of was that explosion in the store; she didn't see Miles come out. She knew Miles wasn't dead. She would have felt it if he was.

"That's the last of them until their backup gets here," Vince yelled out as he reloaded his rapid-fire weapon.

"OK, bet. Spread out, and find the woman. And remember, don't kill her." Ezekiel had a new energy to him. The pain of losing his brother would never go away, but putting down Bloody Hands lessened the hurt.

Rikii heard the order and activated her Flex. She crept her way to a dead authority, removed their magazines, and took their firearm; she then began her reign of terror.

Between the darkness, her Flex, and the carnage lying about, Ezekiel had a tough time pinpointing Rikii.

"Zena, are you still with us?" Ezekiel said.

"Copy," Zena responded through Ezekiel's earpiece.

"Go ahead and Flex. Tell me what you see."

Zena obliged and Flexed—her sight amplified. She could adjust her sight to see up to three miles away and adjust it to be nocturnal and see heat signatures that would allow her to know exactly where Rikii was. "Got her. She's encroaching onto Vince. She's armed as well."

"Exact location, Zena?"

"Coming up on his left at a forty-five degree angle."

"Vince, go ahead and Flex. You're going to be taking one to the head."

"Shit, you didn't have to tell me. I been ready," Vince said.

"When I drop her with the tranquilizer, I need all parties to crash on her quickly," Zeke ordered his remaining men.

But as soon as he finished giving the order, a shot rang out, and Ezekiel saw Vince go down. Zeke wasted no time. He drew his tranquilizer and shot at the direction Zena told him, hitting Rikii.

Rikii dropped and spasmed, her body uncontrollable from the leech-looking bullet digging into her skin. When she came to, she tried to rise but was grabbed and zip-tied. Rikii saw the man she just shot getting up, and the bullet wound in his head was regenerating at an accelerated rate.

Rikii noticed a knife hanging from the hip of one of her abductors. She managed to grab it before being completely zip-tied and stabbed the man in his leg. He went down, hollering. Rikii sliced at random body parts of her abductors. They let her go so they could nurse their leaking wounds; she didn't give them time. The moment Rikii was free, she sliced and stabbed her abductors. Attempting to take her alive was ludicrous, but Rikii took complete advantage of their ignorance.

She focused her attention on the man who came out of the store after the explosion. But she was cut off by a woman, whose eyes glowed purple, and the man that had healed himself from a bullet to the head.

"Sorry, beautiful, but we gotta put you down now," Vince said as he removed his own knife.

"If I was to cut your dick off, would you be able to grow that back?" Rikii asked.

Vince hesitated to answer because he truly didn't know if he could. He looked at Zena, who received the message that it was better for her to take point.

Zena, a few inches taller than Rikii but just as athletic, sized Rikii up. Rikii was slightly fatigued and still in her heels. Zena was built differently; she took pride in her body and shaped it to be a force that even a man wouldn't want to contend with. She did her time in the military but found a better home in this team of misfits. It suited her well. Their motto was simple—only the weak die young. More than confident in herself, she set her firearm down, took her knife out, and went toward Rikii.

Zena thrusted her blade toward Rikii's face, who quickly weaved, blocked the thrust, and swung her own blade at Zena's throat. Zena, Flexing, saw the counter and leaned back, grabbing Rikii's arm before she could retract it, but Zena landed a kick to Rikii's privates.

Zena punched Rikii in the face with her free hand and charged her into an abandoned transport. Rikii felt the pain in her back from the side mirror, but she couldn't focus on the pain. Zena had a tight grasp on Rikii and stabbed at her.

Rikii caught Zena's wrist, preventing the blade from piercing her. Zena was astonished by her strength, but her surprise was interrupted by Rikii biting her ear. Zena screamed and broke away from her. Rikii came in quickly, thrusting her blade under Zena's tactical vest, but Zena sidestepped, making Rikii miss her targeted area. Zena came at Rikii, attempting to stab her arms then her stomach. Rikii deflected Zena's blade with her own as she managed to step back and out of reach from the attack on her stomach.

Zena didn't let up, though Rikii managed to defend her strikes, she quickly assumed her guard, and Rikii did likewise. Zena went to stab Rikii in the face, but she didn't fully extend the strike hoping Rikii would fall for the feint; she didn't. Rikii came at Zena swinging; Zena ducked and kicked Rikii to create distance.

Zena went on the offensive and came in fast, swinging her own strikes. She managed to back Rikii up against the transport again. Zena's last swing went high, aiming for the side of Rikii's head. Rikii ducked and sliced at Zena's thigh. She became irate at Rikii's speed and flexibility. Zena's thigh was leaking blood badly, but she was not fazed.

Zena had her blade up. She approached Rikii, who let her get into striking distance. She went to thrust at Rikii's face, but Rikii was quicker, and she thrusted a strike at Zena's arm, slicing it, and thrusted at Zena's face. Zena managed to lean back and swing at Rikii, who ducked and decided for a leg takedown. Rikii managed to scoop Zena by the legs, taking her to the ground and successfully assuming a full mount before Zena could use her blade to stab her.

Rikii took her blade and drove it into the side of Zena's neck. Rikii twisted the blade and extracted it, blood gushing everywhere.

"Well, fuck me," Vince said as he stood there, astonished at the impressive knife fight that led to his comrade bleeding out.

"You next, baby," Rikii said as she stood up, breathing heavily.

Vince dropped his blade and upholstered his firearm.

"Yeah, I prefer bullets, not blades."

"Alive, Vince," Ezekiel said as he came upon his comrade's side.

The sounds of the oncoming sirens came closer. It was only a matter of minutes before the second round of the authorities' reinforcements was upon Ezekiel and his team. Ezekiel observed the scene. He only had three remaining teammates and saw his dead comrades and dead authorities laid out on the street.

Tia was right. I was going to lose some men to this one.

"Aye, yo!" a loud voice shouted.

Ezekiel turned back toward the store, horrified at the sight of Bloody Hands exiting the store—in one piece.

Miles saw Ezekiel's face and smiled.

"Round two, motherfucker."

17

Miles walked up to Ezekiel, who stood his ground.

"So, what we doing?" Miles asked.

Ezekiel caught his meaning. "Same as before, only hands."

"Good, because it doesn't look like y'all too good with blades," Miles taunted.

Ezekiel didn't entertain the insult but undid his tactical vest and removed it.

What's up with everyone always stripping to fight? Miles thought.

Miles noticed Ezekiel stretching and assumed his guard.

"Zeke, what the fuck?" Vince said.

"Grab the bitch and get her to the rendezvous point. I gotta finish this," Ezekiel ordered.

"Say less," Vince responded.

Miles peered over Ezekiel's shoulder to acknowledge Rikii.

"You good, love?"

"I'm still fucking hungry," Rikii responded.

Miles laughed. "OK, baby. Let me put this fucker in the ground, and I will get you a steak dinner." Miles kept his gaze on Ezekiel. "You ready?"

Ezekiel assumed his guard, revealing the tattoos on his forearms; one arm said "Stay" and the other "Ready."

Miles and Ezekiel fought like two gods: immovable objects meeting an unstoppable force. Miles went flying into a transport so hard that he completely smashed the side of the transport. Ezekiel came upon him, picked him up, and threw him again.

Miles rolled to his feet to meet Ezekiel, who tackled him into the middle of traffic. Ezekiel gained his footing, stood, grabbed Miles by his ankles, and swung him into the windshield of a transport driving by. The driver of the transport had hit the brakes immediately upon impact. Unfortunately, the driver swerved and lost control, =crashing into another transport. Miles apologized to the unconscious driver as he dug himself out of the transport and went back into oncoming traffic.

Ezekiel used his Flex to physically move any transport that got in his way and made his way over to Miles.

Miles swung a right hook that landed on Ezekiel's jaw. He stumbled but recovered and threw his own series of heavy punches. Miles had his Flex activated the whole time, and he felt nothing. His plan was simple: let the strong boy wear himself out before delivering the final blow.

That's the problem with you, newbies. You had no time to train your Flex. Y'all get too tired quickly, but I expect nothing less from second rate. Me, though, I been doing this for decades, Miles thought.

"Damn, just imagine if you were there in the club that night. You might have been able to save your brother," Miles said as he was bobbing and weaving Ezekiel's punches. "Then again, you fight like this. Probably not, though."

Ezekiel became aggravated at the taunts; he could only hit Miles so hard without doing complete damage to his own hands. But Ezekiel had a bigger issue, he was getting tired. Using his Flex this much took a lot of stamina, and he felt himself getting weaker. Miles rushed Ezekiel, both getting hit by an oncoming transport; Miles rose, Ezekiel slowly. More transports swerved and honked at the two men fighting in the middle of the street.

"Is that all you have in the tank, kid?" Miles asked.

Ezekiel walked over to Miles and threw a punch, but Miles caught it in his hand.

"Yeah, kid, I think you're done," Miles said as he punched Ezekiel in his nose, breaking it.

Ezekiel managed to stay on his feet. He activated his Flex and began throwing swings recklessly. Miles let them land, for he retaliated by throwing his own swings, both going pound for pound. Ezekiel became tired, his knuckles bleeding and broken.

"You really woke up this morning thinking you were going to be the one to put Bloody Hands down," Miles said as he punched Ezekiel in his collarbone, breaking it. "Tia sent you into a suicide mission, kid, but I can make your death painless, or I can draw it out." Miles kicked Ezekiel, who was trying to crawl away.

Miles grabbed Ezekiel, flipped him over, and kneeled down beside him.

"Why does Tia want Rikii?" Miles asked.

Ezekiel spit blood in Miles's face.

"Fuck you."

Miles looked next to him and saw a manhole cover that had the word "sewer" written on it. Miles grabbed it and kneeled back over the top of Ezekiel. Transports stopped, and people exited their vehicles to observe the scene. Some people had their PDPs out recording, some honked their horns, and others shouted.

"Last chance, kid," Miles said, looking at Ezekiel's face. His eyes bloodred, his nose disgustingly broken.

Ezekiel stayed silent. He accepted his fate. To bring death to so many and not expect it to come to you was just ignorance.

"I can respect it, kid," Miles said. "I am well aware that there aren't many places for people like us in this world, so I don't take this personally. You had a job to do, and well, you tried. But I do know if Rikii was in my current position, she wouldn't be too happy that you interrupted her while she was eating. So this is for her."

Miles heaved the manhole cover above his head and smashed it into Ezekiel's face.

Blood splattered all over Miles, his eyes widening, his mouth creeping into a sadistic smile as he repeated smashing until nothing was left of Ezekiel's face.

Miles looked up and saw the crowd, horrified at such a gruesome act of violence. He smiled, taking pleasure in them being extremely uncomfortable. Miles stood, covered in blood, clothes full of bullet holes.

Sandy beaches and fruity drinks.

Rikii moved quickly. She easily disarmed and killed the two men left trying to take her, which only left her and Vince. Rikii couldn't Flex just yet. Whatever she had been shot with still prevented her from doing so. She dropped her knife; Vince had her at gunpoint.

"OK, now put these on." Vince tossed a pair of metal wrist restraints at Rikii.

"You come do it," Rikii said.

"Put them on, or I will shoot you in the leg."

"So?"

The sirens were only a few blocks away. Vince couldn't take them all by himself, and Ezekiel hadn't returned yet.

Fuck me.

"Get on your stomach and place your hands behind your back," Vince ordered.

Rikii did not move.

Vince cursed aloud and moved closer to Rikii; his firearm still aimed at her head.

"Damn, woman, who the fuck are you?" Vince asked, taking interest in the woman who single-handedly decommissioned most of his team.

Vince moved in closer to Rikii; he thought it best to approach her from behind.

Rikii only had one shot to make her move. They wanted her alive, and she was using that security to earn victory. Vince approached her straight on and then circled behind her.

Rikii immediately dropped and activated her Flex, hoping it would work, and grabbed the metal restraints and her knife.

Vince was taken off guard; Rikii had Flexed, and he couldn't see her. He fired a shot, hoping that hit her in the head; he would rather not get paid than get dead.

Vince felt a strong blow to the side of his head but stayed on his feet and began shooting from the direction of the hit.

Rikii's Flex had miraculously worked, and she was grateful. She grabbed the restraints and used them as brass knuckles and punched Vince on the side of his head. Rikii quickly moved, anticipating that Vince was going to shoot.

Rikii took her blade and stabbed Vince under his tactical vest. Vince grabbed Rikii, who relaxed her Flex. Rikii held Vince's gun hand up so he couldn't shoot her. Rikii twisted the blade inside Vince's gut, and he yelled in pain. Rikii extracted the blade, then stabbed Vince in his testicular area.

He made a sound Rikii had never heard before and dropped his weapon. Vince fell to the ground, taking Rikii down with him.

Rikii took the blade out and stabbed Vince in his eye, driving the blade deep.

"The name is Rikii, three i's," Rikii said, violently removing the blade from Vince's eye.

"Come on!" Miles shouted at Rikii as she made her way through the streets; he ran toward her and grasped her hand. "The authorities are gonna be on our ass."

Rikii didn't care who was chasing them as long as she was running with Miles. And with that knowledge, she ran through backyards, through traffic, behind stores, and down a couple of alley ways.

"Come on, a couple more blocks, then we are at the light-rail, babe," Miles said.

The sounds of sirens were everywhere. Miles couldn't figure if they were just for him and Rikii or other degenerates.

They got to the light-rail just in time for it to depart. They boarded, and they took a hard look at each other. Miles saw Rikii was sweating, her hair disheveled, her face bruised and swelling, her clothes ripped, and her heel broken. Rikii looked upon Miles, who was covered in blood. His face had black residue, and debris was still in his hair, which was coming unbraided. His clothes were full of holes from the gunshots.

And none of it mattered. They were drawn together like magnets. Miles held Rikii close to him and kissed her.

"There is nothing in this world, and I mean nothing, that will make me love you any less, you understand?" Miles said.

"I understand."

"Why is my sister after you?"

Rikii began to cry.

"Hey, now, whatever it is I can fix it. I promise," Miles said as he wiped away her tears.

That's why Rikii loved Miles—behind the monster was a man who could love like no other. A man who would fight God on her behalf and not think twice. Miles would move mountains; he would conquer the moon if it were what Rikii desired. Miles's love ran so deep that sound reasoning no longer registered with him.

"I need a shower, clothes, and food, and then I will tell you everything, "Rikii said.

Miles smiled.

"Of course, my love. Of course."

18

Tia Graves stared out the window, lost in thought. Her emotions were all over the place. Just three hours ago she watched her father, Augustus Miles Graves Sr., be buried. The myriad of people who showed up was not surprising to Tia. Most of them were business partners and enemies who wanted assurance that he was dead. Tia paid for celebrities to sing and hired multiple pastors to speak at the funeral. During the burial she ordered fireworks that lit up the sky for thirty minutes. She wanted to show the world that this was not a time of sadness but a celebration of life.

She succeeded. Her father's funeral was being broadcast over three major TV networks and multiple radio stations. But only the ignorant took this facade as a celebration of life. Only the smart ones knew all this was for Tia to show her accession to the throne. It was for her to show her father's enemies that there is a new power—and she wears stiletto heels.

But all in all, Tia loved her father, and all she ever wanted was for him to love her back. She did everything in her power to gain his attention and went to the lengths of learning the ins and outs of the foundation.

When she saw that wasn't working, she decided to excel in her university; she made it a point to outdo all the other students. She thought showing her father that his coin was not wasted on her would make him proud; it didn't.

She even took measures of composing the best scientists and tech geniuses, for her father, to help conceive children and implement them with the Nano-Hive. She knew her father loved his Bloody Hands, and he wanted more just like him. So, Tia thought, *What if she could give her father multiple upgraded versions of Bloody Hands?* Maybe then she would be recognized. But where she saw Rikii excel when she assassinated the other trainees, Augustus Graves Sr. only saw disappointment.

In his last moments, there were no last words, just a will that stated how the foundation should be run and how coin should be distributed. Tia poured herself a strong drink and sat herself behind her desk, which was formerly her father's. The office had the best view in all of High-Top, and Tia took some satisfaction that not only High-Top would be hers, but all the Districts. But then despair set in at the thought of Miles still being alive—a thorn that would forever be on her side.

Tia had beefed up security at her father's funeral, just in case Miles and Rikii made an appearance. She didn't inform anyone about the reason, but Styles already knew, and he was not happy. Tia didn't blame him; they both saw the news footage of Miles smashing Ezekiel's face in with a manhole cover. Tia thanked God that it was dark outside, and no one could make out that it was Miles performing the gruesome act.

Tia's PDP rang, and she noticed it was an unknown number. She thought it best to ignore it. It rang again. Tia took a sip of her drink and answered the call, ready to chew someone's head off.

The day of my father's funeral and you people want to fucking bother me.

"What is it?" Tia answered the phone call, but there was silence on the other end. "Hello, who the fuck is this?"

"Do you remember when we were kids and you begged desperately to play tag with Styles and me? I never wanted you to play, but Styles had a soft spot for you. Nonetheless you could never tag me. Even when I stopped running and let you get close enough to tag me, I would shake you off, and just like that, I was out of your reach again." Miles's voice came over the phone.

Tia's heart sank. She had been expecting her brother, but she knew deep down it was Bloody Hands who was paying her a visit.

"Miles, listen, it was a misunderstanding. Can we just talk?"

Miles was silent.

"Did you see the funeral?" Tia hoped to break the silence.

"Styles always let you tag him, though. I guess he wanted you to believe that by doing so you would have fun too, and it made you feel like you were equal to us."

"Miles, I'm begging you. Please, can we talk?"

"I watched you two fools running around playing make believe, and that's when I knew—you and Styles are not equal to me," Miles responded. "I know everything, Tia. I know about my nephew." Miles let it resonate with Tia. "He is a good-looking kid."

Fear had set in. Tia became anxious, and her heart raced. "Miles, listen—"

"I don't listen to a lesser human. I gave you an opportunity to leave us, and you spat in my face. The only reason, and I swear it's the only reason, that you are alive right now is because Rikii made me promise to give you one more chance, for the kid's sake. So this is your final warning. Stand the fuck down."

"Yes," Tia responded, being left with no choice.

"Yes what?"

"What? What do you mean yes what?" Tia asked.

"You were raised with manners. Yes what?"

I hate you; I hate you; I hate you. I fucking hate you, Tia thought.

"Yes, sir," Tia answered, with great reluctance in her voice. Tia stood up from her chair with her drink in her hand and stared out the window to the elegant view.

"And Tia..."

"What?" Tia roared, but her frustration was cut short by the shattering of her drinking glass. Tia flinched from the sudden impact and noticed her window was starting to crack. She examined the cracks that were forming from a hole, realizing it was due to a bullet.

"It's that easy," Miles said as he hung up.

———•·•———

The sky was blotted with beautiful trees of assorted colors, signaling the season. The District of Kings City was very remote from the other Districts and shared little of city life. Roman was lowered in his raft from his main air transport. He stepped out and observed the men who were well dressed, holding rapid-fire weapons in front of a large black gate embellished with a large letter R on it. Roman had cleaned himself up since his night at Roxy's in New Area; he was not too happy to get his skin sewed up as it brought up questions that he was definitely too embarrassed to answer.

Dressed in a chartreuse suit, he approached the guards, who gave Roman the signal to stay where he was.

"What's your business?" the guard said with all seriousness.

"I'm expected," Roman answered.

"Your business?" The tone of the guard now came across as very annoyed and impatient.

"I am here for the meeting."

"Your name?"

"Roman."

Roman watched one of the guards speak into an earpiece while still holding his gaze with Roman. The guard, satisfied with what he was told over the radio, signaled Roman that he could approach. The other guardsman touched his watch, which controlled the black gate.

"Remain still," the guard ordered Roman as he used a handheld device to scan Roman. The device discharged green illuminations that made a horizontal line in the middle of Roman's stomach, and in unison, part of the line went up while the second went down.

"Scan complete. Welcome, Roman." The guard escorted him half-way through the driveway.

The house was up on a hill, and Roman had to be escorted by another guard, who then ushered him to the front door of the house, which was also guarded. The house was modernly designed, the windows were enormous, and blinds were absent. The inside was not a home occupied for living purposes.

Roman entered the house and was instructed by a maid, a good-looking one, to follow her. She guided Roman to the dining room, where there were more Shifters sitting at a table. Roman made his formal greetings to them before taking his seat at the table.

"Are we ready to commence?" Roman asked his companions. They all agreed in one accord.

Roman double-tapped the table, and it illuminated with different screens and instructions. He fiddled with the screen and pressed one final button, which caused their chairs to mechanically recline. When each Shifter was comfortable in their seating, a headset manifested itself from behind each chair. A cable with a sharp end ejected from the headset of the chair, and each Shifter changed into their metallic state. Each took the sharp end of the cable and pushed it into their skulls, where their metallic skin withered away to showcase a fabricated brain. They stuck the sharp end into their cerebral cortex, where it then all went dark.

The Shifters all awoke in a fancy hallway of some Victorian mansion. The marble floors complemented the enormous white marbled staircase. The white walls were adorned with gold decor, gold lights, and statues of figures of a different time. The windows were gigantic and made one wonder who had the courage to climb to clean them. They were now in the in-between, a holding place between the consciousness of their metallic forms and their true forms.

"Welcome," an affluently dressed man standing at the top of the staircase greeted. He was of reasonable height, pale-skinned with a head full of neatly dressed black hair and reading glasses.

"Our Father," all the Shifters said in one accord.

"It seems that the lands in Rae are finally in our possession," the man said.

"Yes, sir, it seems that Tia Graves is making good on her end of the deal," Roman informed.

"I would like to interject and bring knowledge of Roman's failure to kill Bloody Hands," a woman said. She was tall, pale-skinned, with blonde hair and blue eyes. "Leaving him alive will be a danger to our plans."

Roman looked at her emotionlessly. "You think you could have done a better job, Amelia?"

Amelia was another Shifter who had a vendetta against anyone who had the potential to excel her. Her beauty was only simply to cover up her evil self. Mechanical body or not, she would sell her own parents to get ahead and be recognized for it.

"Without a doubt," she said, giving Roman an arrogant gaze.

"I have it on best authority that Bloody Hands will not be a problem for us unless we give him reason to be a problem," said a male voice. He was of average height and had the face of a teenager. He, too, was pale-skinned, his hair black.

"Ah, finally a voice of reason. Thank you, Kalib," Roman responded.

"Enough," the man on top of the staircase ordered. "Why must my children always have to fight?"

"Sorry, Father," the Shifters said in unison.

"We must prepare ourselves, with the districts under our thumb, securing the lands in Rae definitely will secure our position in Kurtaz. We already have some feet on the ground in the Free Territories. How good my influence there will be is still up for debate. Ever since the Water Wars, my position with the families has alleviated." There was a slight pause before he continued. "Well, you all have your parts to play. Now go and make your puppets dance. Our guests are arriving."

The doors swung wide open, and men and women finely dressed piled in. They received alcoholic beverages as they made their way into the mansion, conversing among themselves. Roman smiled at the Shifters piling in for their quarterly meetings, which was more of a gathering.

"Tread lightly, brother. Amelia has her sights on a bigger prize, and she is not afraid of walking over you to get it," Kalib said.

"Oh, trust me, I know our sister all too well. Nothing ever changed," Roman responded.

"And I know my brother, and I know very well you're not letting Bloody Hands go that easy, ain't ya?" Kalib asked.

"He made a fool of me at Scotts Beach and at some shitty nightclub. You damn right I am not letting his ass go," Roman said.

Kalib toasted his brother with his wine glass. "Happy hunting."

Roman fell into a dark state and immediately awoke, struggling for air. He was confined to a small pod that had no room, turning only to remain still on your back. He opened his eyes and clawed at the glass that kept him from exiting the pod. He knew what it was, and he did not want to be there. He tried to yell out, but his sounds were muted when the glass quickly slid open.

Black metallic tentacles grabbed his naked body out of his pod and lifted him up. His body frail and his eyes weak, Roman still managed to observe his surroundings. He saw thousands of pods neatly stacked in columns that went so far, there seemed to be no end to them. Each pod held human bodies that were frozen, while their consciousness were in the shifting bodies, enjoying their reign out in conquered worlds.

"Roman," a tired voice said.

Roman looked up and saw the source of the tentacles that had him restrained. Fear had gripped him, and he knew his facial expressions revealed it. The Our Father was lifted with his tentacles, and he was at eye level to Roman. His body frame was skinny, his skin was grey, and the marks on him resembled third-degree burns. Hair was absent on him, and his eyes were a cold blue.

"I am disappointed in you. Your failure is a disgrace to the Ryse. You were once again outmaneuvered by mortal beings. You make my design seem inferior to the beings of this realm," the voice said.

"No, Our Father, your design is perfect. I just misjudged the situation. I didn't expect them to survive this," Roman explained.

Our Father hovered high over Roman, his tentacles tightening around him. It pleased Our Father to see the fear in Roman, for it reminded his children that in the end, they are still mere mortals.

"Roman, spare me your babblings. Humble yourself before me, and I will ignore my pride and give you another opportunity to be in my good graces."

"Our Father, thank you for your mercy. Thank you for forgiving me of my weakness and my negligence." Roman cried out.

Scan QR Code to listen.
Str8 Drop
by
M.U.R.K Entertainment

PART THREE

19

The snow began its slow descent down from the night sky onto the District of High-Top. Natives busied themselves, using their PDPs or conversing with their peers as they moved up and down the streets. High-Top was a marvel at night—its myriad of holographic billboards illuminating, its skyscrapers, which were home to many corporations, and its entertainment life, especially at night, fooled many to come live in such a district. People would spend their days working two or three jobs just to make ends meet, and for what? Was it for validation to live in such a district?

"Um, Miles?" Rikii spoke, hoping to break the awkward silence. They were standing on the sidewalk for about fifteen minutes, looking up at one of the holographic billboards.

Miles heard Rikii, and he wanted to sound comforting, but he couldn't. "You should have let me just kill her."

Rikii sucked her teeth, shook her head, and looked away from Miles. She wanted to apologize to make him feel somewhat better, but she knew her judgment call was right.

"I get it, though. Someone has to raise the fucking kid. But the next time I see Tia, it's one between the eyes." Miles continued to stare at the billboard.

"Where do you think they got it from?"

"It's an up-to-date photo, so who knows. Tia could have taken it back when we were in the hospital in New Area or a security camera somewhere. I wouldn't be surprised if it's from the bodega."

"What's the plan?"

"The plan?" Miles paused. "The plan has been the same from the get-go—we need to get the fuck out of the Districts. And after that we can do whatever we want to do."

Rikii stood in front of Miles, sized him up, and took his hand. "We will figure it out, but we should head back and sort it all out. Plus, I'm really fucking cold."

Miles stood there, still fixated on the billboard, donning a pair of flashy spectacles with clear lenses, a stylish blue winter coat with gray jeans, and black boots.

Tia really had the balls to pull this shit. How in the world did God bless that evil bitch with a kid? But God also blessed me with love. This world truly makes no sense, Miles thought.

"Yeah, let's head back. We need to meet Dimitri about our vouchers so we can peel the hell outta here," Miles said.

"Why do you think she used my face and not yours or just both of us? I mean, I know where the skeletons are buried as well," Rikii asked.

"Yeah, that's the part I can't figure out, but we are not fortunate enough to have time to ponder it," Miles said as he turned to leave.

Rikii stood her ground and turned to look once more at the billboard. Her face was on the billboard in a holographic state, being rotated with the word "Wanted" written in a banner underneath it. She was wanted for the violent murders of authorities in the District of New Area.

Heavy smoke and the aroma of strong liquors suffocated the casino, but business was doing well. Card tables, slot machines, and roulette tables were full, with the joys and the greed of the citizens of High-Top. Young and middle-aged women cuffed themselves to men in cheap suits to feed their own need for validation. Men laughed, and some drank their sorrows away as they spent their child's tuition money.

Miles stood in the middle of the aisle. There was no need to find a hostess; he would be approached by the right people in charge. Standing in the middle of a casino with a chip on your shoulder is good enough to get some attention.

The casino's security guard, more like Dimitri's henchman, approached Miles and signaled him to put his hands up. Miles did so, and the henchmen patted him down, locating Miles's firearm, which he holstered on his right thigh.

"You will get this back when you leave," said the henchman.

"Aye, there's my guy!" A pale-skinned male, slightly under six feet, sported a fitted purple suit with nothing but his bare chest under the blazer. His pants came above his ankles, revealing no socks with his expensive dress shoes. He kept his hair shaven and maintained his masculine cheekbones but kept his signature curled mustache.

"Dimitri," Miles acknowledged him, but he made sure his tone was understood that he was in no mood for Dimitri's overly animated personality.

"Come on, follow me," Dimitri said, smiling as he walked through the casino and greeted everyone he walked past.

They walked up the stairs and down a hallway occupied by henchmen dressed casually.

"In here," Dimitri informed Miles. "Can I get you something to drink?"

"You can get me my vouchers," Miles responded.

"Oh, wow, right to business, huh?" Dimitri sat behind his desk, two of his henchmen on both sides. "Please sit," Dimitri said, gesturing to the chair in front of Miles.

Miles sat, and there was another henchman behind him, which was an intimidating tactic wasted on Miles.

"So there has been a change of plans when it comes to the vouchers. Um, the price you paid was good all the way until they started flashing your girl's face over every billboard and on every news network," Dimitri said.

"How much do you want?"

"Well, see, it's not a matter of coin," Dimitri said in his playful tone as he corrected Miles.

Miles showed no emotion.

Dimitri nodded to the man behind Miles, who placed a formidable metal briefcase on the table. Dimitri fiddled with the briefcase; it had a biometric lock on it. It sprung open, releasing cold vapor, and Dimitri pulled out a container filled with glass tubesof green liquid and placed it in front of Miles. "You know what those are?"

"No."

"It's called Juice. It's the new hot shit on the streets now. It temporarily amplifies a person's cognitive abilities and physical abilities by like tenfold. People can study better, pass every fucking exam, and as far as strength goes, well, I tell you, the skinniest guy can bench over three hundred. And by the gods, people are paying with their kidneys for just one of these things."

"What's this gotta do with my vouchers?"

"Well, my new price for the vouchers is that you obtain more of this for me."

"Yeah, I'm good. I'll find someone else."

Dimitri leaned back into his chair and crossed his legs. "Yeah? Who? Who the fuck in High-Top can you find who produces better vouchers than me? You might find some teenage prick who can give you a knockoff version of my shit, but once they see your girl's face, they are either gonna rat you out or not do business with you at all. That bitch is the district's most wanted, next to Bloody Hands. And let's face it, catching him is like trying to catch a cloud."

That bitch? Miles thought.

Dimitri leaned forward and pushed the container closer to Miles. "This is payment for the vouchers and my silence."

"I see. Well, where am I supposed to get you more of this Juice?"

Dimitri clapped his hands.

"I thought you would never ask." He pulled out his PDP. "So the Wong family in the Free Territories created Juice and successfully kept it off the radar of all governments. But they knighted, on this side of the Districts, Bruce to be distro."

In holographic mode, Dimitri enlarged the whole District of High-Top and swiped through multiple Districts, showing Bruce's reach throughout the districts.

"Motherfucking Bruce, that toothless old-timer Long story short, we used to be associates way back when, but you know how people just fall out," Dimitri said.

"In my experience, men fall out over pussy or greed."

"Shit, even both, right?" Dimitri laughed at distant memories. "Well, nonetheless, I need his supply, and then I can prove to the Wong's that I'm better suited to distribute."

"And you can't do this yourself?" Miles asked.

"I could, but then I would lose men, and why do that when I can send someone else?"

"I see, and let me guess, you and your lil goons here have probably been hitting Bruce's earners wherever and whenever you can, making it hard for him to sell here?" Miles pointed to the metal briefcase on the table. "And my guess is that is how you probably got that case."

Dimitri looked at his two henchmen, bemused.

"How the fuck would you know that?"

Miles leaned in. "Besides having no product, you wanna know what else Bruce has that you don't?"

Dimitri lost his humor and became serious.

"Well, chest out, chin up, big boy."

"An airstrip," Miles said as he let his words sink in.

"I am one for jokes and busting balls, but I ain't catching the punch line here," Dimitri said, his patience running out.

"He can move so much product because he flies and drops the containers at certain drop points. You know, places people wouldn't look, or he pays rent to some Joe Blow who allows him to drop on his property."

"And how the fuck would you know that?" Dimitri asked.

"No, no, Dimitri, you're not thinking outside the box. The punch line is why the fuck would I need your vouchers when Bruce has air transport and a pilot who can maneuver undetected through the sky?"

Dimitri's eyes widened as he felt a hand rest upon his shoulder. He saw well-manicured nails and a blade at his throat. His henchmen were ghostly white, as they were astonished to see Rikii appear out of nowhere. The henchmen gained their composure quickly and aimed their weapons at Rikii, who stood behind Dimitri, ready to slice at Miles's command.

"OK, OK, we can work this out," Dimitri pleaded as sweat beads dropped from his face.

Miles stood up, and he smiled, ignoring the henchman who held a firearm aimed at his head. "I tell you what, you tell your boys to put their weapons on the table, and we can talk it through."

"Put your goddamn guns on the table!" Dimitri ordered his men; they obliged.

Miles winked at Rikii, who winked back; Rikii sliced Dimitri's throat, quickly grabbed one of the firearms on the table, and shot and killed both henchmen next to her.

Miles turned to look at the man who held him dead to rights. The henchman was still in shock. "I want no prob—"

Rikii shot him in the head.

"Yeah, I met with Bruce. I actually owed him a favor," Miles said looking at Dimitri's dead body leaking blood all over his desk.

"More is about to come. I'll meet you in the front," Rikii said.

Miles held Rikii by her waist and kissed her on the lips. "I'll see you at the front. Go give 'em hell, baby."

Rikii went to exit the room.

Miles looked at the desk and noticed the metal container and the glass tubes of Juice. He put the valves back in the container, closed it, and took it with him.

"Sandy beaches and fruity drinks," Miles said aloud as he went to exit the room.

"We ain't finished here, Bloody Hands," Dimitri said, his voice was not his own but of that of a scorned woman.

Miles turned, and with shock, saw Dimitri lifting his head, blood gushing from his throat. His henchmen also began standing up, their pupils completely white, both men fully dead.

"It's time to make good on your contract," one of the henchmen said, standing as if someone else had lifted him from the ground.

Miles's heart began to race. He had his Flex ready in case someone tried to attack him, but how do you fight the dead?

Miles ran out of the room and into the hallway, but he stopped in his tracks when the walls started to bleed. Endless amounts of blood poured from the walls onto the floor, and Miles found himself ankle-deep in blood. He went to lift his foot, but a hand under the blood grabbed him.

"Aah, what the fuck?" Miles yelled as he kicked himself out of the grasp.

More hands emerged from the bloodied floor, grasping and pulling Miles. They multiplied quickly, wrapping around his throat and waist, tugging at his clothing and hair. Miles used all his strength to break away, but the hands were too strong. He managed to reach for a firearm hidden from security and shot at the grasping hands and arms, but it did no damage. They continued to drag him down, clawing at his face and torso. Miles succumbed to their will, and the hands covered his mouth and his eyes, only darkness available to Miles.

Miles woke up, with no knowledge of how long he had been passed out. He lay on his stomach, and when he opened his eyes, he was looking into the eyes of a dead man lying perpendicular to him. The man was an older man, pale-skinned, wearing only swimming trunks, and blood ran down his forehead from a bullet wound. Miles quickly got to his feet; he was outside in a pool area of a hotel resort littered with dead bodies, several floating in the pool. Miles looked into the lobby, where smoke and fire were fiercely protruding, and saw more people lying about, dead.

"I see you finally woke up," a woman said behind Miles. He recognized the voice; it was the same voice that he heard from Dimitri and the henchmen. Miles turned to look at the older woman, who was pale-skinned. She dressed in casual wear, decorated with blood, her makeup running with blood around her mouth. She smiled, showing only bloodied gums from teeth that had been violently extracted from her.

"You again, huh? And you're supposed to be who this time?" Miles asked.

"You don't recognize your own prey?" She answered his question with a question.

Miles shrugged his shoulders.

"Where the hell am I?" Miles asked.

The woman walked past Miles, and like a coroner, she examined the bodies that were in her radius. *"Amazing, you and you alone killed all these people. Like seriously how do you do it? How can you blow half of a resort sky high and gun down pedestrians and still sleep at night?"*

"What do you want?" Miles asked again, his patience wearing thin.

"I want you to remember." The woman stood and spread her arms wide. "I want you to remember all this."

"Scotts Beach. Yes, I fucking remember it. What about it?"

My father got inside information that leaders of a shadow government were meeting with their families to discuss future terrorist operations. Rumor also had it that one of their prospects was an all-out assault against the Graves Foundation. I just got to them first, Miles thought.

"It's time to make good on your end of the deal."

Miles was silent, waiting for her to finish.

"I want you to kill all of them," she said.

"Who?"

"The fucking Ryse. Kill all of them, and stop the fucking breach," she said, her tone even more sinister.

"You know what's funny? My daddy also had a hard-on for the Ryse, and I am going to tell you what I told him: I don't give a fuck. Now send my ass back."

The woman stepped closer to Miles, showing her toothless smile.

"You want to know what Rikii thinks when you make love to her?" The woman grew, becoming the same height as Miles; she leaned into him and whispered into his ear. *"Her thoughts are: She loves you more than her own life. She gives you the keys to her soul with every thrust you give her. She feels so safe and secure with you. I could only imagine what her thoughts will be when I cut her tongue out of her mouth for the hundredth time or gouge her pretty eyes out, and then allow my horde*

to have their way with her until my heart is satisfied. My heart is never satisfied."

Miles was frozen. He couldn't move an inch. The sudden imagery the woman painted struck him with fear and anxiety. "What is this breach?"

The woman grabbed Miles by the jaw and forced him to look into her cold dead eyes.

"Good boy. That is the attitude I am looking for, and the next time you talk to me without respect..." She licked Miles with her bloodied tongue *"I will taste blood."*

The woman released Miles and stepped away from him. *"The breach is the Ryse's ultimate goal. It needs to be stopped, and time is of the essence. But to stop and fight the Ryse, I need Bloody Hands. This current version of you won't cut it; you're soft and sloppy. So I need to whip you back into shape. I'm going to take Rikii, and you can have her back as soon as the contract is fulfilled."*

"What? No! She didn't do anything. And if you want this shit done, I'm going to need her help anyways."

"She's a distraction. Look at you, always so damn emotional over her. Trust me, I'll keep her breathing, but when she goes to sleep next, she won't wake up for a little while."

"Don't...please don't."

The woman walked past Miles and shrugged. *"Because there is only a little kindness left in my heart, I suppose I can make an exception. But only if you show good faith right now."*

"What do you want?" Miles asked.

The woman stood in front of Miles. She stepped to the side, and out of nowhere, Tia and her son Zheff were on the ground, scared. Tia held Zheff with dear life and looked at Miles with pleading eyes; ignorant of the woman standing there.

"Miles, what the fuck? I didn't do anything. I left you alone. Please, not Zheff...not Zheff...please...please," Tia begged.

"What the fuck you want me to do?" Miles asked.

The woman materialized a firearm that only required one hand to grip. She smiled and handed the weapon over to Miles. *"What was it that you said? If I see Tia again, it's one between the eyes.'"*

"Sorry, sis," Miles said as he pointed the firearm at Tia and shot her in the head.

Miles handed the weapon back to the woman, and she looked at him in confusion.

"I want Bloody Hands...the kid too," the woman said.

The woman's toothless smile widened as she looked upon Miles's face of despair. To kill your own sibling was nothing, people did that every day. But to kill a child...a child that belonged to your lover... Now that was a different challenge. Miles was at war within himself as he looked at Zheff, who was on the ground, fear in his eyes. What made matters worse was he could see the resemblance between Zheff and Rikii, and it drove him mad.

"Do it!"

Miles pointed the firearm at Zheff, and tears fell from his eyes.

"Fucking do it! Give me Bloody Hands!"

Miles's hand shook with adrenaline.

"I swear upon myself that if you don't shoot that little shit, Rikii is mine!"

Miles placed his finger on the trigger, and for the first time ever in his life, he closed his eyes to death.

———— • ↠ ————

"Mr. President, your two o'clock is ready," the young redheaded secretary reminded President Floyd.

"Thank you, Diane. You can send her in," President Floyd responded.

President Floyd looked into the small mirror on his desk to check his straight white teeth and his gray hair. He adjusted his red tie and made sure his desk was clean while Diane escorted Tia Graves through the door.

"Mr. President," Tia greeted.

President Floyd kept his manners. He stood up, greeted Tia, and invited her to the brown leather couches in the middle of the well-decorated office. Tia, dressed professionally, obliged, sat down, crossed her legs, and waited.

She took in the scenery of the office. The district's flag resided in the corner, a giant framed photo of the district's first president hung on the wall. There were a few artifacts within the office. In a glass display case was a sword from the olden days. In another case, there seemed to be an armor worn from the warriors who were defeated in this land, way before Tia's and President Floyd's grandparents were even thought of.

"Are you thirsty?" the president asked as he poured himself a drink.

"I'll pass," Tia responded.

"Well then, to what do I owe this pleasure," President Floyd asked as he sat across from Tia.

"Where do you stand on making me general in the next election?"

"Always to the point, aren't ya, Tia?" President Floyd asked.

"I personally gift wrapped and delivered Kurtaz to you," Tia said.

It was no surprise that President Floyd wanted Kurtaz—their resources were the hottest commodity in the world. And none of Floyd's predecessors ever came close to exploiting them.

"Run me through it again," President Floyd said as he sipped his drink.

"My father, may his soul rest in peace, had an incredible hard-on for the Ryse—"

"The Ryse, Lord have mercy, don't even get me started on those leeches. Every way you turn, those bastards always have their hands in something. For a secret society, they're not so secret, just fucking annoying," Floyd interjected. "Sorry, I didn't mean to interrupt." He signaled Tia to continue.

"Well, back in the day my father secured lands in Kurtaz. And for some odd reason, the Ryse has been trying to get those lands ever since. But you know my father. He was unmoving. But I never shared the same optimism for those lands, so it was easy for me to let it go."

"Those lands, I believe it was in Rae, correct?" President Floyd asked.

"Correct," Tia responded.

"If you're going to be my general, Tia, it is crucial that we are up front with everything. Just in case something comes up in the future, we can already have a plan in place."

"Ask what you want to ask me, Mr. President."

"Are the rumors true? Was Augustus creating weapons against humanity and even experimenting with human trials?"

Tia stared at him. "False. Those lands were nothing more than holding sites for our pharmaceuticals."

The president held Tia's gaze. He didn't truly believe her, but he decided it was best to not push the matter. "OK, well, good, but please continue more on Kurtaz."

"I agreed to sell the lands to the Ryse for a low price if they agreed to finance a terrorist faction to invade Kurtaz."

President Floyd damn near spat his drink out of his mouth, "That was you?"

"Yes, it was me. And to make sure they didn't hire incompetent nomads, I planted my own team into the faction. I pulled them out after a couple of years for other matters that I'd rather not discuss."

"Shit, Tia, you just broke so many laws that if anyone besides me hears about this, you will never see the light of day."

"My father taught me never to go into battle with a dull blade." Tia let her words linger for a moment.

President Floyd didn't need to question her, the message was transparent, she has something on everyone.

"I made a deal with Omar Hasaan that I will supply him the weapons he would need to win the war."

"And Sovereign Supreme Amir Saad and the rest of the Kurtazian government were in one accord of this deal?" Floyd asked.

"Of course not. It was a completely backdoor deal. The weapons I will give him will not only help win the war, but it will help with the resignation of Amir and his regime. And if any other assistance is needed, I would be obliged."

"In exchange for what?" President Floyd's interest became more acute.

"That our partnership will be a robust collaboration for five years."

"So you created a war with an outside enemy just so you can cause chaos from within. Because that's what it will be once Omar attempts to remove Saad." Floyd mentioned.

I created the war as one last fuck you for the man who couldn't even say he loved me, Tia thought.

"And in all that confusion, a new government trying to be established would be the perfect time for the Districts to come in and be the glue that holds the country together," Tia said.

"And Omar is going to be holding the door wide open on your order," President Floyd said as he pieced together Tia's plan.

"You're welcome. But let me remind you that the door only opens when general is in front of my name."

Fame and glory would follow Floyd's name for generations if he was to be the president who secured Kurtaz. President Floyd stood up and held out his hand, and Tia stood and grasped his hand.

"You will have my full backing in the election," President Floyd said as he shook hands with the devil.

20

Way, Way, Way Back in the Day

Buddha looked to the sky, closed his eyes, and tried to gain his composure. His head was throbbing from Grool's punches as it felt like he was banging his head against metal. Buddha looked down at Grool's dead body, smiled, and turned to retreat to his men.

Buddha walked back, his head clouded. He wanted to lay down somewhere and rest his body. His brother always told him that he couldn't be a warrior forever. It was better to retire before a younger, more ambitious man in battle retired you with a blade in your gut. He didn't think much of what he would do once he hung it all up for the second time. He didn't know how he was to manage living in an empty home since his wife left him. And if he was going to be honest with himself, living alone while the ghost of his son haunted him did not sound pleasurable.

There has been openings to be an instructor at the academy who teaches the boys how to use tact and weapons. All his choices had one common denominator—he was going to end up hating life regardless. If he had it his way, he would at least want to see her again. The shining woman with no name, she would appear randomly to Buddha, and like a puppy dog, he was at her leg. They would talk for a brief amount of time, but she made it seem like those few minutes were lifetimes. To have her again and his son back would be heaven for him. He hadn't seen her for months, though, and it ached his heart. It took the drive out of him to seek glory. Even his brother was able to see his depression, which wasn't hard when you share the same face. But how would one sound explaining that he was depressed because a shining woman with no name hadn't appeared to him in a while? Buddha usually explained his depression on the loss of his son, an excuse that was more true than anything.

"My lord!" Buddha's warriors shouted, all of them deploying their shields without Buddha's order.

Buddha turned, and with horror in his eyes and in his heart, he watched Grool stand up. He stood, blood covered his body, a light in his eyes. Not life, but an illumination that took root in his pupils. Grool's skin began to shift, as if he were trying to come out of it. Metallic spikes appeared, and within seconds, his appearance changed. What now stood in front of Buddha was a spiked metallic giant, eyes illuminating. Grool's people stood by, spears in hand, not moving a muscle.

Buddha wasted no time and he commanded his men. "Charge!"

Grool laughed, not his normal laugh, not a human laugh, but one that sounded like a machine. Grool leaped high in the air and landed amid the royal military, unarmed but ready to fight. He swung his fist, a ball of spikes, shattering the shields and impaling the men of valor within seconds. Buddha watched his men take swords to Grool, but nothing pierced. Buddha found his own sword, grabbed it, and charged Grool.

Grool paid Buddha no mind, ripping men apart left and right like they were branches. Swords struck him, but he felt no pain, picking one man up and slamming him so hard his body burst upon impact with the ground.

Men screamed in pain and fright.

Grool bent to a runner's stance, and in one motion, his body of metallic spikes spun like a rotor. He ran, shredding anyone within radius of him. Buddha dove for the ground as Grool ran past him.

Grool quickly stood to punch Buddha, but Buddha was already up, delivering a swing to Grool. He caught the sword in his spikey hand. Buddha tried to wiggle it free, but Grool's newfound strength wouldn't permit it. Grool snapped the sword and threw the blade.

"Buddha Bane, where is your might now? Your skills, your confidence, have they failed you?" Grool's voice was evil and machinelike.

Grool hit Buddha, knocking him back twenty yards.

What in the hell is that thing?

Grool came at Buddha again, ducking Grool's swings and extending his short blade using his Nanos. Buddha successfully pierced Grool where his heart should have been; it did nothing. Grool formed a long spike from his hand and attempted to stab Buddha, but his armor absorbed the blow.

"Ark! Ark!" Buddha yelled into his forearm, hoping that his communication went through.

"To the Ark!" Buddha yelled at what was left of his men. They all ran while Buddha's Great Ark descended from the sky. Grool didn't chase. He laughed at them as the blue illumination absorbed them back into their aircraft.

———— • • ————

"Did you really have to do that?" Augustus Graves Sr. said as he walked up to the hideous woman.

"I had to make sure the weapon you built for me was still good quality. Besides it's not like they are actually dead. My scare tactics are inhumane, but they are effective," she said.

Augustus, wearing a nice suit and looking thirty years younger, scanned the dead bodies in the pool area. "I told you he can do it. You should have just trusted me."

"Trust you?" She looked at him with anger. "I trusted you, and look where we are now. Look at me! Look at what they are doing to me!"

Augustus had no words; he only had shame. He wished he would have been stronger and wise, but he couldn't change the past.

"And your daughter..." The woman shook her head in disgust. "How the fuck do you not see that she was in bed with the Ryse? And here I thought you loved me."

Her words shook Augustus. "I do love you more—"

"Then how do you let them do this to me?"

Augustus knew she was right, he ignored Tia's ambitions. He knew he was not a good father, but in his sickness, he could only focus on priorities, and Tia was not one of them. Tia sensed the lack of focus on her and decided to have her own agenda. Many times, Augustus thought about telling his children the truth, what their true purpose was, but he shot down the idea every time, believing it would undo all his hard work and sacrifice, and hinder his true goal.

The woman abandoned her look and morphed into her true essence. She was still hideous—her skin lacking pigmentation, her eyes yellow, her hair balding, her breast sagging, fingernails missing, and her teeth rotten.

She used her power to transport Augustus and herself to a field of tall, beautiful grass. The myriad of trees stood, colossal, and surrounding them were fields of beautiful flowers.

Augustus breathed in the fresh air, and the air was so pure that he could taste its flavor.

"Where are we?" Augustus asked.

The woman walked a few paces, and Augustus followed. Augustus could hear people running to and from as they smiled, having no care in the world. Women, men, and children were dressed in little clothing as if they were unaware of their nakedness. They held hands, they hummed melodies, and they were all living in pure bliss.

Augustus saw a gold illumination in the clouds that slowly descended from the sky. He saw her, his lover, in all her glory, wearing transparent clothing, her skin golden, her hair black and curly, and four wings protruded from her back. Augustus watched her hug and kiss all those who came up to her. She allowed the children to play with her feathered wings. And the woman sung to them, making them all pause and sway to her beautiful voice.

"They were babes when I arrived here. None of them knew how to dress, wipe themselves, or even feed themselves. My assignment was to guide them and nurture them." The woman said as she looked on the distant memory with lustful eyes. "I showed them the way for centuries, and soon my assignment ended. But they needed me. They wanted me, and I couldn't bring myself to leave them. They worshipped me, and I never corrected them. I became addicted to the glory and the praises. And because of those desires, I trespassed ineptly. I loved my realm. I loved my worshippers."

She transported Augustus and herself to another memory. It was dark. He saw dead individuals lying in the fields. He knew from his time from a warrior what carnage looked like. But he knew, from personal experience, nothing was eviler than the slaughter of a people who never knew how to defend themselves. There were no weapons among the dead, no warriors, no champions, just dead men, women, and children.

"Somehow knowledge of the power greater than mine got out, and teachings of this religion had spread," the woman said.

Augustus looked at the woman, who looked on in pure disgust.

"I was their mother. I gave them food, clothes, medicine, marine knowledge. I gave them healthy babies. I answered their prayers. I sung to them. I made myself visible to them. And yet they betrayed me. They lay down with another. I was to be their lover, NOT A GOD THEY CANNOT SEE!"

"What did you do?" Augustus asked.

"I taught my followers how to create weapons. I taught them how to use them, and I ordered them to kill anyone who worships anything other than me. I purged this realm of all knowledge of religions, idols, and gods." She spoke angrily.

"You must understand, in the end, I realized what I had done, and I asked for forgiveness. But I was not granted mercy. I was too tainted. That is why the Ryse is here. They are going to swallow all of us because of my sins," she said as tears of blood ran down from her eyes.

"So, Miles is this realm's last hope. If he fails, we all perish, and the deal that you and I had made will be void," Augusts said, his voice void of emotion.

21

Tia was exhausted, the last couple of weeks made her feel overcome by fatigue. From dealing with her brother's mess, then burying her father, meeting with President Floyd all while trying to be a decent mom was a lot for her to balance. She was supposed to take Zheff to a cinema, but she forgot paperwork in her office and told Maria, her nanny, to take him.

I promise I will take you to the next one, Zheff, Tia thought.

She made a mental note to stop off at the store and buy him some designer clothes and a game or two. She knew buying materialistic things wouldn't substitute for her presence, but it showed that she still cared and tried. Tia was glad that she came into the office late. There was no one to disturb her, and she could work diligently and quietly.

She walked down the hallway to her office, took out her lanyard with her ID, and swiped it to enter. Tia was astonished to see Miles sitting behind her desk. She flinched as her office door slammed behind her; Rikii relaxed her Flex.

"What the fuck y'all doing here?" Tia asked.

Miles was dressed in a black turtleneck with a brown trench coat and black slacks,

his hair neatly braided.

"Did you report Rikii to the authorities?" Miles asked, comfortable in his father's desk chair.

"See, I knew you were going to think that shit was me." Tia walked to the window. "You see this here? The fucking hole you put in my window. Why the fuck would I report her to the damn authorities? Just so all that shit can blow back on me and the foundation?" Tia paced back and forth. "I have a better fucking question, knowing she's public enemy number one, why are y'all still in the Districts?"

Miles didn't buy her response, but he wasn't here for a confession.

"The Ryse," Miles said.

"Am I supposed to fill in the blank?"

"The deal you made with them, the one that involves Rae. I need you to abandon that deal."

Tia laughed. "First off, fuck you. Second, that deal is already done. Why the fuck you care?"

"Because it's bad news if they acquire those lands."

"Miles," Tia's spoke as if talking to a child, "we mined that whole fucking jungle for resources for at least two damn decades. We took the oil, minerals, fruits, trees, and everything. Under the ploy of a mining institution, we constructed a haven for our ungrateful children." Tia sized Rikii up and down. "There is nothing left there. If they want a fucking wasteland, let them have it. Now get the fuck out my office."

"You think I'd risk coming here for you to tell me no over a fucking wasteland? I need you to give me everything you have on the Ryse right now."

"I have nothing on the Ryse, Miles."

"Who did you have contact with when making the deal?" Rikii interjected. She was dressed the same as Miles but with heels decorating her feet.

"Oh, she speaks," Tia said. "Maybe you should go talk to your son. You know, be a fucking parent for once."

Rikii backed down, and Miles noticed the change in her demeanor.

"The breach," Miles simply said.

"The what?" Tia asked, her attitude was clear.

"Did Dad say anything about the breach and the Ryse?"

"No, boy! Now get out of my office!"

"Styles, where is he these days?"

"Do I look like his master? Why would you want him anyway?"

"Dad could have told him something. You know he was always fond of Styles," Miles said, letting the truth of his statement sink in; a little revenge for Rikii.

Tia felt the insult, but she controlled her rage.

"Miles, listen, and listen to me carefully. I don't know what shitstorm you are in, and quite frankly, I don't give a rat's ass. Leave my office, don't contact me ever again, and for our name's sake, get the fuck out of the districts."

Miles and Rikii made their way to the door.

"Rikii," Tia said, "you can stay. It would benefit Zheff to have both his parents in the picture. Or you go with Miles, and I'll just let Zheff know you abandoned him again."

Rikii, in her rage, turned and went to lash out, but Miles grabbed her and ushered her out of the office.

"Fucking bitch," Rikii said, frustrated.

"Can't blame her. She is her father's child," Miles said.

They walked down the hallway, thankful it was after hours, making it easy for Rikii to move undetected. They approached the elevator and waited for its service. Miles noticed Rikii was still frustrated, and he wrapped his arm around her.

"You want to talk about it?" Miles asked.

"It's so hard to talk about. You don't understand the pressures I have dealt with."

"You right, I don't understand, but I want to understand." Miles turned Rikii so she was facing him. "Make me understand you." He cupped Rikii's face in his hands.

"I want to be his parent, Miles, but I don't want to lose you. I have to pick between you two, and the choice is so hard, yet I have been choosing you. And I'm happy when I'm with you, but I still feel like shit. And then I think if I chose Zheff, would I be happy? What if I'm happy and still feel like shit when I'm with him?"

The elevator door opened, and Miles and Rikii stepped inside.

"Tell me how to fix it, Rikii," Miles said.

"I don't know, Miles, right now we have other shit more important than my problems."

"Your problems are my problems, and they come before everything," Miles said.

I'm happy I didn't tell you that an ugly woman who I had made a deal with made me shoot your son just so you wouldn't be put in a coma. That would have added a lot more stress to you, Miles thought.

The elevator stopped to open for other passengers, Rikii quickly activated her Flex.

One man was waiting, a young man in his midthirties but looked tired. His skin was a lighter tone with black curly hair, and he dressed casually. He stepped in the elevator and did a double take.

"Sorry, I thought I saw someone else in the elevator," the man said.

"Whoa, must have been a long day, I guess," Miles said with a friendly smile.

The man looked at Miles, and with astonishment, he recognized him.

"Miles! Oh, I mean, shit, Mr. Graves! It's good to see you, sir."

Miles looked at the young man with a blank stare.

"I'm Javon, Javon Richards. I recognize you from the photos from the funeral service. Sorry about your loss. What brings you here at this late hour?"

They showed my fucking photo at the funeral? Wait, Dad had family photos?

"I had to see my sister. Her workaholic ass can never be found, so I figured this was the best place and time to sneak up on her."

"True. Facts."

"So what the fuck is it you do here?" Miles asked.

"Yeah, your boy is the head of real estate," Javon said excitedly, happy with his title.

Did he say head of real estate?

The elevator doors opened, and Miles and Javon walked through the main lobby, engaging in small talk.

"Aye, you get down out here?" Miles asked.

"My professional answer is no," Javon replied.

"Do I look professional to you?" Miles stated.

Javon took a moment to think and took a gamble.

"Yeah, I get down. You need me to recommend a spot?"

"More like accompany me," Miles said.

"For real? Shit, OK, OK, my homeboy throwing a little something at his pad, his shit be legit. If you tryna roll through, I can vouch for ya."

"OK, let's make it happen."

Javon was right. The party was legit, whoever Javon's friend was. It was a rooftop party with a heated pool outside that had a decent view of the District of High-Top. Women were running naked outside, jumping in and out of the pool. There was a bar and two bartenders doing an excellent job at keeping people spirited with liquid courage. Inside the luxury apartment, there were men and women dancing to the loud music, people snorting drugs off the counter or someone's chest, and people smoking cigarettes and just having a good time living in the moment.

"So what you think?" Javon asked as he drank out his plastic red cup.

"Yeah, y'all get down all right," Miles responded. "I noticed these people look young."

"Well, yeah, they're mostly from the universities or people who love the nightlife."

Javon studied Miles from his hair down to his shoes.

"So I've been trying to figure it out," Javon stated.

"What's that?" Miles had to shout over the music.

"If you are older than Tia, then you gotta be in your forties, right? Like how the hell do you look thirty?" Javon shouted back.

Miles smiled. "I just turned forty-seven, and age ain't nothing but a number. I simply decided to not get old."

Miles realized Javon was not listening but focused on the beautiful women that were on the sofa inside the apartment. They were dressed promiscuously, which apparently was the fashion trend for this party, but they were beautiful. One of the females was tanned, pale-skinned, long dirty blonde hair with green eyes and a giant tattoo that came up from her breast to her throat. The other was light-skinned, her braids, like Miles's, came to her shoulders, her eyes were brown and her makeup exquisite. Both females were eyeing Javon and Miles, trying to engage them from a distance.

"Well, come on. Can't keep them waiting," Javon said as he pulled Miles with him to the sofa.

Miles knew Rikii was present, and she was not going to be happy about this.

Miles, Javon, and the girls engaged in conversation; Miles's charisma had everyone laughing. He continued to buy drinks for them and made sure Javon's cup was always filled.

The two women's attention was on their PDPs for a moment, and Miles took the opportunity to talk to Javon.

"Aye, so how long have you been head of real estate?" Miles asked.

"About two years now."

Good.

"Let me ask you a question," Miles said.

"Shoot."

"The lands in Kurtaz, specifically Rae. You know anything about that?"

"Well, I know we recently sold those lands," Javon responded and downed his cup.

Miles signaled a guy to bring more drinks. "Sold them to who?"

"Um, I believe it was some power company. FPE, some shit like that." Javon received his new cup and began sipping it.

A power company.

"Yeah, FPE. It stands for Forever Powered Energy. Yeah, they are based out in butt fuck nowhere in the Free Territories and a few other places around the world. Shit, now that I think of it, I believe we have one out here in the Districts. New Alexander, I think it's where it's at."

"Oh, I figured. I just wanted to be sure. I appreciate it," Miles said as he laid back on the sofa and pondered his thoughts.

Well, I'll be damned. We can't stay in the districts, with all eyes out for Rikii. We can check in with the Wongs in the Free Territories, and we can move from there.

The music changed to some dance music that made everyone in the party go crazy. One of the females, whose braids were similar to Miles, turned to Miles and kissed him. Their make out session was not even two minutes before Rikii pulled the young woman off Miles.

"He is taken, honey, go fuck off," Rikii said to the woman. The woman had a look of disgust on her face as she got up from the sofa and minded her business elsewhere.

"Yo, girl. What the fuck is your problem?" Javon asked, aggravated at Rikii for ruining Miles's good time.

"It's all right, Javon. I prefer her anyway," Miles said looking at Rikii, who had a look of pure irritation written on her face.

Rikii began dancing in front of Miles, swinging her hips. She sat in his lap and grinded on him. Her butt deliberately rubbing against Miles's manhood. She leaned her face back, mouth perpendicular to Miles's ear.

"You know I will kill every bitch in here," Rikii whispered.

"It was just business, babe."

Rikii kept slowly grinding. She took Miles' hands and made him feel her breast and her privates. "I have business that you can handle."

Miles chuckled. "Yeah, I bet you do."

"Did you get what you came here for?"

"Yeah, looks like we are going to be taking a trip to the Free Territories."

"Why?"

"It seems like the Ryse could be hiding out there so we shall see."

"Yeah, about that, Miles. We need to talk." Rikii adjusted herself to where she was sitting on Miles's lap. "You never explained to me why the fuck we are chasing them if we barely made it out alive against Roman."

Rikii looked at Miles, who was reluctant to open his mouth. "When I came back for you in the casino, babe, you looked spooked.

You were on the floor in the hallway looking up at the ceiling like you seen a ghost or something."

Miles knew it was only a matter of time before he would have to come clean. He wouldn't be able to operate knowing that he was keeping secrets from Rikii; she wouldn't allow it regardless.

"When we get out of here, we really need to talk," Miles said.

Rikii saw the frustration and the slight fear on Miles's face. She never forced anything out of him, and she wasn't going to start today. Whatever Miles was holding back was hard for him to tell her. She decided to help loosen him up, as it could facilitate his words. Rikii began kissing Miles's neck.

"Well, then, we should enjoy our night." Rikii licked Miles's ear. "Can you do momma a favor?" Rikii whispered, feeling Miles getting erect.

"Of course," Miles whispered back.

"Go find that bitch who was kissing you. I want her to come back with us," Rikii said lustfully.

22

Tia controlled her breathing as she pushed the dumbbells from her chest. She had been in a morbid mood for the last week, and the only thing she could do to not think about it was to lose herself in fitness.

She dropped the weights, stood, and looked at herself in the mirror. She was fit, her strength and conditioning routine twice a week facilitated her need to keep focused, while her other hobby of self-medicating kept her relaxed. She figured it was a good enough balance; no one was perfect.

She saw Styles enter the state-of-the-art gym that in the foundation's building. Tia was impressed that her emergency call caught him so off guard that he didn't have time to dress in one of his tailored suits. Instead, he just wore a gray sweat suit with white sneakers.

"Why you call me here?" Styles asked.

"Well, hi to you too," Tia replied. She sat down on one of the workout benches and took a swig of her water bottle.

"I was in the middle of something, Tia."

"Were you fucking?"

"No."

"So if you weren't in between legs, then what were you in the middle of?"

"That's none of your business."

"That fancy condominium you live in, the fancy transports you drive, the suits you wear are all provided by my foundation, so everything you do is my business. If your fucking, I want to know what the bitch looks like. I want to know how tight her pussy is."

"Are you back on the droppers?" Styles asked. "You're only a bitch when you're on droppers."

Tia took a slight pause and decided to shift the conversation. "Forever Powered Energy."

"Mm-hmm."

"Why do you think they wanted the lands in Rae? I mean it's a wasteland now."

"Tia, who cares? We had a deal. They upheld their end, and we upheld ours. What's done is done."

"Yeah, it's just...I feel like shit ain't adding up."

"Listen, we have President Floyd's attention. You're close to being groomed for general. I have people already on the ground creating your campaign and politicians begging for us to accept their donations. Why the fuck are we worrying about used-up lands?"

"Because Miles and Rikii paid me a visit."

"What the fuck?" Styles yelled out as he stood from the flat bench in frustration.

"When, Tia?"

"Last week."

"Last week? Tia, Rikii is the most wanted person in the fucking Districts, and she was here? Someone could have seen her."

"Oh, hush, Styles. You know damn well they ain't stupid enough to get caught like that. Now sit your ass down."

Styles sat, and Tia allowed him to gain his composure.

"Why were they here?" Styles asked.

"Initially to question me if I was the one who delivered Rikii's name to the authorities."

"Well, that would've been foolish."

"That's what I told them. But then the convo switched to the Ryse. He told me to back out of the sale."

Styles stayed silent.

"You and I both know they are the ones behind Forever Powered Energy, but what I can't get out of my mind is why Miles is interested in them. He even asked if Daddy had info on them."

"Listen, Tia, we need to distance ourselves as far away from them as possible. Whatever mess they are in, we can't be attached to it."

"No fucking shit. But I am curious, what do we know about Forever Powered Energy and the Ryse?"

"Tia, who fucking cares. You ain't care then, why care now?"

"If I'm going to be general, I need to know these things."

"Not these things."

Tia looked at him like he was crazy.

"These are dangerous people."

"We are dangerous people, Styles."

We don't even hold a candle to them, Styles thought.

"Something you want to tell me, Styles? Something I need to be worried about?"

"Yes, fucking with these people can cause big fucking problems."

"I want to look more into them."

"I don't recommend it."

"Good thing I don't fucking work for you. Put a team together. I want to be updated on the who, what, when, why, and how weekly."

Styles was not happy with Tia's demands, but she held the key to the Districts, and he needed to play his part.

"Sure, Tia." Styles got up to take his leave. "I hope you reconsider this, though."

Tia smiled at him as he left the gym. She couldn't ignore the feeling in her gut, but she was not ignorant of the fear that was in her heart.

23

"Are you sure this plan is tight?" Rikii asked. She sat on the bench next to Miles as they spoke, and people watched.

"It's the best I got right now."

"And this connect of yours, can you trust him?"

Miles looked at her. She was wearing a cropped black hoodie with black baggy cargo pants and sneakers. She kept a pixie haircut but abandoned the finger waves. She was still so gorgeous, and her black makeup added more intrigue.

"I only trust you," Miles said.

Rikii looked back at Miles and rolled her eyes at him. Ever since Miles had to explain himself on why they had to stop, the Ryse, and what he had to do to her son to keep Rikii safe, there had been some distance between them.

"His name again?" Rikii asked, her attitude was clear.

"Finesse."

"That's his birth name or..."

"Does it matter, Rikii?" Miles showed his impatience.

They sat on the bench in silence as they let their eyes wander the streets of the Free Territories, which were completely different from the Districts. The Districts were filled with skyscrapers and enormous apartment buildings, and in a clutter of people, the Free Territories offered more of a sense of peace. The palm trees, the old construction homes that people decided nothing was wrong with were tourism-worthy. The Free Territories sat by the ocean, so every restaurant was in competition for the best seafood dishes.

Miles tapped Rikii on the shoulder to show that there had been a four-door transport parked and flashing its headlights at them.

"It's probably him," Miles said as he stood and walked over to the transport; Rikii followed.

"Miles, baby!" Finesse roared as he exited the transport, with his arms open for an embrace; Miles didn't entertain it. "Oh, you're still a brute after all this time."

Finesse was Miles's height, dark-skinned, and slim. He wore men's clothes, but his stature allowed him to wear them tight enough to where it looked good on him. He kept his wavelength haircut low with a hard part, and he wore expensive black glasses.

"And by the gods," Finesse took off his glasses. "Who might you just be?" Finesse asked, looking at Rikii.

Rikii held out her hand to greet him. "Rikii."

Finesse grabbed Rikii's well-manicured hand and kissed it. "Finesse, forever at your service for all your needs and wants."

Miles watched the exchange in silence. His face didn't show it, but he was annoyed.

"So, Rikii, do you belong to him?" Finesse asked, pointing at Miles.

"Honey, I belong to no one." Rikii spoke in her soft-tone voice.

Finesse looked at Miles. "So I can?"

"Finesse, you touch her again, it will be the last thing you touch," Miles said, his voice filled with annoyance.

"Jesus, OK, I get it. At least I asked," Finesse said. "Well, come on. Get in. We gotta drive."

They arrived at a beautiful white home that was connected to the other homes of the same caliber; it seemed like that was how the whole neighborhood looked.

Finesse walked up the porch and opened the front door. "Come on, I'm on the top floor."

Miles and Rikii followed. The house was a three-story apartment building with two apartments on each floor; Finesse reached his door and went in.

"I was expecting glamour," Rikii said aloud.

"Oh, then you would love my home back in the Southern Isles," Finesse said.

"Ah, I see. So you're just passing through?" Rikii asked.

"Indeed. Now cop a squat so we can get started. I know Miles to be one to get right to business," Finesse said.

The apartment was a small one-bedroom living area. The couch was old and mediocre, but it didn't stop Miles from making himself comfortable on it; Rikii remained standing.

Finesse grabbed his PDP, turned on holographic mode, and showed an impressive image of Forever Powered Energy.

"So as you already know, FPE is a multibillion coin industry. They have infrastructure all around the world. Their main building is in the Districts, New Alexandria. They have at least four data centers on the west side of the Districts and two on the east. But you already knew that. What you paid for was the data collection center here in The Free Territories..." Finesse changed the image. "And boom."

Rikii looked at Miles. "You paid him to get information?"

"Yes, I didn't have the time to do it myself because I was too busy trying to get you out of the Districts."

"I didn't know I was such a burden," Rikii whispered under her breath but loud enough for Miles to hear.

"I didn't say you were," Miles shot back.

"How much did you pay him?" Rikii asked.

"A lot, hence why this info better be worth it."

"Guess leaving me in the dark is becoming your new pattern now," Rikii said.

"Rikii."

Rikii held up her hand to Miles, signaling she was done talking.

"Children, can we get back to it now?" Finesse asked.

An image of a bald, pale-skinned man showed up on Finesse's PDP.

"This is Robert Low. He is your data manager for the data center here in the Free Territories. He's married with three kids, all teenagers, each one an entitled piece of shit."

"Finesse," Miles said with a tone that meant get to the point.

"Yeah, so our boy, Robert, only portrays as the family man on family holiday cards. He has a mistress and has a decent drug habit."

"What's he using?" Rikii asked.

"Droppers, pills, herb, venom...you name it, he on it."

"Send me the details of his mistress and his dealers," Miles requested.

"Yeah, there's one more thing, Miles. He's protected by the Council," Finesse informed.

"Seriously? Which family has their hooks in him?" Miles asked.

"Well, it seems he's buddy-buddy with Matteo Maximo."

"Fuck," Miles whispered to himself. "OK, well I have a plan for that. I have a report with the Wongs, so I'll check in with them and convince them to help me convince the Council to let their guard down."

Miles looked at Finesse, then back at Rikii.

"What?"

Finesse walked to the closet and brought out a few duffel bags and placed them on the table.

"Here is what the rest of your coin got you," Finesse said.

Rikii was first to move toward the table to unzip the bags. She noticed that one of the bags had small firearms and simple handguns that a teenager could get.

"No rapid-fire weapons. No shotguns. Like, what the hell are we gonna do with this, Miles?"

Miles rubbed his temples in frustration. "The barons were child's play compared to the Council. When we move, we gotta move in silence. Damn near everyone here in the Free Territories is affiliated with a family."

"I know how the Council works. Ain't my first time here, Miles."

"Then why the fuck are you asking stupid questions?"

Rikii's mouth hung open. He never spoke to her like that even when he used to get aggravated with her in the beginning of their relationship. Miles realized the words and tone he used were not supposed to escape his mouth, but he was too exhausted to practice restraint.

"Well, I'm going to take my leave. You two obviously have some issues, and either way you slice it, sounds like you two are about to stir up crazy shit here in the Free Territories. So, yeah, I'm out," Finesse said flamboyantly.

"Don't you stay here?" Rikii asked, confused.

"Girl, I told you to come check out my spot in the Southern Isles. This place is what Miles also asked me to secure, along with the rinky-dink transport outside," Finesse said as he tossed the keys on the table. He took his leave.

"I'm going to bed," Miles said as he got up from the couch to walk to the bedroom.

"We visit the Wong's when I wake up."

Rikii didn't respond; she unzipped the remaining two duffel bags. She was intrigued by the clothes stuffed in each bag; one bag for her, and one bag for Miles. She scavenged through her own bag, liking most of the apparel, and she gave Miles his credit for always knowing her sizes.

24

Dressed in a satin robe and comfortable slippers, Arthur Wong stood by his pond. He reminisced back when times were easier for himself. The luxury of being a son to a councilman meant ridiculous amounts of concessions. His youth was not wasted on books or learning the ins and outs of the family business.

He chased women, drank, raced transports. Hell, he even traveled the world with his entourage. He got into his fair share of brawls; his size gained him advantage in most of those fights. In his father's final years, members of the Wong family began making plans on who would be next to sit on the Council. Arthur's father warned him one night that the families were losing their way. And soon the Free Territories wouldn't be so free anymore. Something drove Arthur to promise his father that he would not let the Wong family be led astray. What prompted him to promise that? It was probably the alcohol he always made sure he had in his system.

Nonetheless, Arthur took things seriously and began following his father's footsteps, bound by a promise that was made when he was tipsy. Not one soul thought Arthur would accomplish what he has thus far, but it was still safe to assume that Arthur Wong would be more content being somewhere else other than here.

Arthur was so lost in thought that he didn't hear Miles walk up behind him.

"You're losing your touch," Miles said as he stood next to Arthur.

"It appears I have lost a lot more men for not doing their jobs."

"Eh, you really can't blame them," Miles responded.

"I guess you're right."

There was silence between both men. Arthur was completely thrown off guard by Miles's arrival, but his demeanor didn't show it. Miles observed the fish that swam freely throughout the pond.

"You know I owe everything to your family. You saved my family and my reputation. When I became head of the family, I sat on the Council. It was hard for me. I wasn't accepted by the Council, and my own family didn't see me as a leader. But I did my best. I eventually earned respect. But when your father reached out to me to partner on Juice, it changed everything. Your father even gave me full rights to it as long as I promised to push some of it on the streets in his selected locations. Fuck, he even facilitated a deal with the Xing Nation, who bought it from me for so much coin that no one in my family can ever doubt my position again, not even the fucking Council," Arthur vented. "And my condolences for your father as well."

Miles nodded and just listened. Arthur hoped that giving credit to the Graves was enough ass-kissing to keep the beast in its cage.

"I am going to cut the bullshit, Arthur. Robert Low, shit bag who runs Forever Powered Energy, he's cliqued up with Maximo."

"Are you asking me or telling me?"

"I'm telling you that I want you to convince Maximo to cancel their protection on him."

"Miles, I can't do that."

"That was the wrong response, Arthur."

"Miles, we ain't talking about no average civilian here. Robert has been with Matteo Maximo for years. They came up together from school days for fuck's sake."

"Well, I am pretty sure Matteo would love to hear about your Juice business."

Arthur gave Miles a hard look.

"I know the deal between you and the Xing Nation hasn't been finalized, a shame if there is disruption at the manufacturing site."

"Really, Miles?"

"You have six hours."

"What the fuck can I do in six hours, Miles?" Arthur became irate, his face red. "This is not good business, Miles."

Miles got into Arthur's face, and Arthur shrank in size, his temper deflated, and ego crushed; the beast was out of its cage.

"Do I look like a fucking businessman, Arthur? Do I look like I draft contracts and sign off on checks? Look around your home. I decorated your walls with the blood of your guards because that is what the fuck I do."

In truth, it was Rikii who did the legwork, but Arthur didn't need to know all that.

Arthur held eye contact with Miles; he was too frozen to do anything else.

"You got me twisted, Arthur. You think I'm asking you to help me with Maximo because I fear the Council? Nah, nah, this is me being courteous. I'll go to war any day with any of you fucks, but I'm short on time and even shorter on patience." Miles spoke in a cold, low tone he learned from his father. "Six hours."

Miles took his leave and left a speechless Arthur to his assignment.

———— · ————

The man crawled the best he could, bleeding profusely from his right wrist, which was missing a hand, and suffering wounds to his back. One moment he was playing cards with the boys and the next, they were attacked.

He crawled with fear and adrenaline, sounds of his compatriots fighting and dying rang out. Blood soaked the floor as he crawled through it and over the fallen. He came upon another fallen lying on his back with a knife in his eye. The man searched him and found a handgun underneath.

The injured man thought if he could get to the exit, he could force himself to stand and run like hell. His plan was thwarted by a heavy foot that pressed on his wrist. He yelled in pain and spasmed. The tanned foot was decorated in a high heel, with manicured toes. The man looked up and followed the heeled foot to a leg attached to a beautiful woman wearing a red cheongsam.

"Oh God, please," the man begged for his life. He dropped the handgun, hoping she would show him some mercy.

"I said keep at least three of 'em alive, Rikii. What if this dumbass doesn't know shit," Miles said.

"You will figure it out," Rikii said. She took her foot off the man and stalked off.

Miles, irate at Rikii's attitude toward him, couldn't help but watch lustfully as she walked away. Dressed in fitted black slacks with leather suspenders, Miles rolled the sleeves up on his black button-down and turned the man over on his back.

"Do you know who we work for? You are a fucking dead man!" the man shouted.

"Oh, I know who you work for, and I don't give a fuck. You wanna live?"

The man nodded yes.

"I hear you're Robert Low's dealer. Or one of you were," Miles said as he scanned the room of dead bodies.

"His dealer is over there," the man said as he nodded to his left.

Miles saw a man sunken to the floor with a blade protruding from his heart.

For fuck's sake, Rikii.

"But I can get you whatever you need. I can get you the same shit he gets," the man begged.

"What does Robert really spend his coin on?"

"He loves to shoot up venom, I can get you that shit. But I hear he has been trying to kick the habit. He even checked himself into a rehab months back. He usually sticks to low doses of the droppers."

"I want the venom he shoots into his veins," Miles said.

"I can get that for ya. We got it here."

Miles motioned him to stand up and retrieve the drugs.

The man wrapped his bleeding wrist with some of his clothing and stood. He walked wobbly, having lost so much blood. Their headquarters was a dry cleaners, and they hid their drugs in the customers' clothes. The man made his way to the clothing conveyor and pressed a button.

"OK, right here," the man said as he unzipped a garment bag and dug into a pocket of someone's pants. He pulled out a small glass bottle of liquid and handed it to Miles.

"This is all you got?" Miles asked.

"How much do you want?"

"Enough to make someone's first trip their last one," Miles replied.

"That's enough in your hands. If you plan on giving it to someone who is used to it, then you definitely going to need more. But a first-timer, that whole bottle...shit, even half can kill them."

"Well, then, I think I can manage with just this. I appreciate your help."

Miles grabbed the man and quickly snapped his neck before he could think about anything.

Miles walked out of the dry cleaners and spotted Rikii outside, tired of her attitude. Miles decided to just keep walking and let her catch up, if she decided to still want to follow him.

25

Robert was lost in pleasure as he thrusted his mistress. She was a beautiful forty-year-old, whose sexual hunger increased with her age. He had a fist full of her black hair and another hand on her shoulder, both way too lost in their ecstasy. Rikii watched him for a couple of minutes before relaxing her Flex.

"Boo," Rikii said, relaxing her Flex as she pointed her small firearm at Robert and his mistress.

Robert flinched hard and fell off the bed, while his woman screamed loudly as she rolled off the bed.

Robert sized Rikii up—all-black hoodie, black denims, boots, and driver's gloves. Robert thought with her stature, she was nothing more than a pretty face with a weapon. He got up, prepared to fight; his plan shattered when he saw Miles in all black, walking up behind her with his menacing smile.

"Going somewhere, Mr. Low?" Miles asked.

"On the bed now," Rikii ordered the woman, who quickly obliged.

"If you know who I am, then you know my connections. You are a dead man," Robert said.

Miles pulled out his PDP, and showed it to Robert. He looked confused at first but realized he was meant to read what was on the screen.

You have the green light,

Wong.

"That is a message from Arthur Wong, stating that the Council, mainly Matteo, has dropped you from his protection list." Miles saw a chair and made himself comfortable; Rikii held Robert and the woman at gunpoint.

Robert Low's disposition had changed.

"I have coin. Give me a number, and I will get it to you in fifteen minutes."

"We don't need your coin. You can walk away from this safely. All you have to do is answer some questions." Miles pulled out a small toiletry bag.

Robert watched him remove two syringes. Miles took one of the syringes and stood. He looked around the room, found Robert's pants and removed the belt, then made his way to the woman on the bed.

"Give me your arm."

"Please, I have nothing to do with whatever shit he has going on," the woman said, scared.

"I wasn't asking," Miles said.

The woman gave Miles her left arm and he put the belt around her arm. He searched carefully for a vein, and once he found one he was content with, he inserted the syringe and pushed the venom into her. In mere seconds, the woman fell back onto the bed, her high was clear.

"Man, I've been clean from that shit," Robert said.

"So I have heard. That's a real accomplishment," Miles responded, going back to the chair. "So about my questions..."

"Man, I really don't know too much."

"Sure you do. It's about FPE."

"OK, sure. What you wanna know?" Robert asked, shivering from his nakedness.

Miles fiddled with his PDP.

"Before we begin, I will need you to state your name and your job profession. And oh, just in case you already didn't realize, if you don't cooperate, Rikii here is going to blow your brains all over the wall, then I will be forced to ask your wife these questions. And if she can't answer them, then I will have to ask your kids. We clear?"

Robert nodded.

"OK, let's begin. Your name and profession."

"Robert Low, data collection manager at Forever Powered Energy."

"And what data do you collect at Forever Powered Energy?"

"Data on energy."

Miles was silent for a moment.

"What else do you collect?" Miles asked.

Robert looked at him, bemused, and Miles responded with a nod to Rikii. Rikii pointed her firearm at Robert's head.

"We...we collect...um...we collect data on the habits of the populace."

"Elaborate that for me, please."

Robert knew he was a dead man the moment he revealed what they wanted to know. His family was doomed regardless, but what choice did he truly have? He could at least be alive to get his family into hiding.

"We collect information on people. We collect data on their phone conversations, who they text. We watch the net and see what people research. We collect data on fashion and music trends, and we track it all."

"And what do you do with this data?"

"Nothing. We just collect."

"So this information has never been used to gain advantage in any circumstances?"

Robert thought about lying, but something in his gut told him that this guy already knew the answers to the questions he was asking.

"The war in Kurtaz. We were able to collect data and help perform certain conclusions on how their military was operating."

"And that's how the Invaders have been kicking their ass for five years?"

"Yes."

"But there aren't any data collection centers in Kurtaz. So how is that possible?" Miles asked.

"FPE silently bought Kurtaz's largest energy company and implanted our technologies. We planned on building a base in Rae soon."

"Do your investors know you do this?"

"Some."

"So data collecting is the new modern day warfare now, huh?"

"I guess. I don't know," Robert answered.

Miles scratched his chin, pretending to be thinking of some elaborate question.

"How do you know all this?" Miles asked.

"It's my job to know. We can't collect the data we need if the manager doesn't know what to collect."

"So all data managers across the company know about this?"

"Yeah, basically."

"Well, what about the employees you supervise? Do they know?"

"They are ignorant. They don't know that the tech we use is collecting the other data. The only ones who would know would be only a few shift leaders. They all signed nondisclosure agreements during the hiring process, so they don't talk."

"You do know everything you are doing is illegal, right?"

"I just work there. I don't make the rules. None of it was my idea. I honestly thought, when I got hired, we were just dealing with energy."

"So who makes the rules? Whose idea was it?" Miles asked.

"I don't know, man. The CEO's, I guess. I don't know. I just do what I am told."

Miles fiddled with his PDP once more.

"OK, Robert, that's enough questions. I think I got all I need."

"Are you going to let me go?" Robert asked.

Miles stood with the syringe and belt and tossed it to Robert.

"Yes, of course, but I need you to shoot that into your arm first."

Robert grabbed the belt, wrapped it around his arm, and took the syringe. He kicked the habit once, he could kick it again if it meant survival; he shot the venom into his arm.

Miles and Rikii watched him fade away into his high as he slouched naked against the wall.

"Are you going to let him live?" Rikii asked.

"If he survives that, then he is meant to live. I added some droppers to the venom, which should be enough to kill him," Miles said.

26

"So now what?" Rikii asked as she sat in the passenger seat of the transport.

Miles smiled mischievously.

"We turn the tables."

He pulled out his PDP and pressed a button that played a recording of Robert and Miles's conversation.

"What are you going to do with that, Miles?"

"Well, he basically admitted to treason, war crimes, espionage, and a shitload of other shit that FPE shouldn't be doing. So once the world hears this, the populace is going to hang them for us."

"Wouldn't that put a big target on the Graves Foundation? They sold lands to them that can come back to us. Shit, they might even retaliate," Rikii asked.

"Maybe, but I don't really care," Miles responded.

"Well, I do."

"Why?"

"Why the fuck you think why?"

Tia and Zheff, Miles thought.

"Okay, I get it, but there is no other play, my love," Miles said.

"There has to be, Miles."

Miles shook his head, unable to find words that Rikii wanted to hear.

"Miles, you upload that. I'm not sure if we are going to be able to survive that."

"Don't worry, babe, I won't let anything happen to you," Miles said as he placed his hand on Rikii's knee to reassure her.

"I'm not talking about that, Miles."

Miles looked at her quizzically.

"What are you trying to say to me right now?"

"Our relationship will not survive. You upload that, you are putting a target on my son's back, and you would be betraying me for a second time."

"The fuck you just say to me? Betraying you? When the fuck did I ever betray you? I have been nothing but more than loyal to you. I don't know how many times I need to apologize to you, but everything I did was to protect you. I don't see that as betrayal," Miles said, his tone serious.

Rikii remained quiet, still shocked that the words came out of her mouth.

"You would fucking leave me after all we been through? What we have, you're just gonna throw away for what? A kid you don't know, a kid that was conceived through manipulation." Miles fiddled with his PDP. "Yeah, I don't think so."

Rikii watched him as he began setting up the process to upload the video to news networks and other platforms. She reached for the PDP, and Miles grabbed her arm.

"Miles, I swear, you do this, I'm leaving."

Miles paused, anger and irritation flooding him. Everything he had done since he met Rikii was for her.

"Rikii, you need to stop threatening me. I would never say words like that to you," Miles said as he released Rikii's arm.

"I'm not threatening. I'm promising," Rikii said as she hit Miles in the face, then reached for the PDP again.

Miles took the hit to the face but held on to the PDP. He needed to restrain Rikii, and in his annoyance and irritation, he grabbed Rikii by her throat and pinned her tightly against the headrest of the passenger seat.

"I have a responsibility, Miles. Zheff didn't ask to be here and doesn't deserve to be a target."

"And we do? What the fuck did we do to deserve to become fucking weapons? Last I checked, we ain't asked to be here either." Miles let his words sink in. "I'm not entertaining your bullshit. I'm going to upload this recording and save your life."

Miles released his grip on Rikii and uploaded the recording.

Rikii exited the transport and began walking away; Miles got out as well.

"Rikii! Rikii! Get back in the transport! We can't be out here!" Miles yelled.

Rikii ignored him and kept walking. Miles ran up behind her to grab her, but Rikii quickly turned and punched Miles in the face.

What the hell? Miles thought as he checked for blood.

"Don't fucking touch me! I ain't playing with you, Miles."

"Where are you going to go?"

"It's no longer your concern. Goodbye, Miles."

Rikii activated her Flex and continued to walk.

"Wait! Wait! Rikii, please wait!" Miles roared, panic in his voice.

Rikii stopped and turned to look at Miles. Even though it was night, she could make out the look of panic on Miles's face like a mother who couldn't find her child. It pained her to see Miles like that, so she decided to offer mercy and let him say his peace; she relaxed her Flex.

Miles tried walking to her, but she signaled him to not come closer. He could lose her at any moment; she could Flex, and he wouldn't see her again.

"Rikii, please stop," Miles said, his hands out, pleading. "I need you. I can't live without you. You are my reason. You are my whole world."

Rikii remained quiet, looking away from Miles, trying to mask her tears.

"I fucked up, Rikii. I made a decision that I shouldn't have, and I am so sorry. I don't know what you want me to do."

"I didn't want you to upload the damn recording!"

"Rikii, I made a vow to you. You remember what they were?"

Rikii knew, but she didn't want to respond.

"We were in the heat of the moment. We were on a job. We were outnumbered, and we had to shoot our way out. We both ran out of bullets, and it became hands on. After it was all over, I saw you covered in blood, and I asked you to marry me," Miles said. "You told me if I gave you my vows right now, you would give me yours, and that would seal our union."

"Stop, Miles," Rikii said, the memories flooding her.

"As long as I draw breath, I will give you my everything. Every day I will give you my all." Miles slowly encroached Rikii. "You are safe here. Your thoughts are safe here." Miles pointed to his heart. "Your emotions are safe here. Your strengths, weaknesses, your dreams, your secrets all safe here." Miles pounded his chest. "Here is your home." Miles stood close to Rikii. "You remember your vows to me, Rikii?"

Rikii looked Miles in his tearing eyes. "You are free. Here, you are free." Rikii pointed to her heart. "You are free to be yourself. Here, you are free to love. Here, you are free to hide, you are free to cry, you are free to be happy. Here is your freedom. The only chains around you are the ones that bind our hearts."

Miles stood in front of Rikii and placed his forehead on hers, his tears flowing like a river. They were a union, and Rikii's pain was his.

"Stop apologizing to me, Miles. You have nothing to apologize for," Rikii said. She took a deep breath. "I was never upset with you for what you did. I understood completely the position you were in. I felt your pain, Miles. I felt your guilt of what you did. I felt your fear of what would happen once you told me. I felt it like it was my pain, my guilt, my fear. Then I grew angry. I grew angry at whatever that thing is that put you in that predicament. Then I grew angry at you, Graves, for fucking creating us because we are monsters. And Zheff is nothing like us, and the world knows it, but it refuses to let him be innocent. The world refuses us to make something good here because we are monsters created for destruction."

Miles guided Rikii to the curb, and they sat down as he consoled her and listened to her words.

"You know, sandy beaches and fruity drinks sound a lot more interesting with my nephew present," Miles said.

"What?" Rikii was puzzled.

"Fuck this world, fuck the foundation, fuck Tia, fuck my dad, fuck whatever devil orchestrating all this shit. I'm with you, and with you I have my freedom. So I'm done. No more Bloody Hands." Miles gently kissed Rikii on her cheek. "Let's go do some good. Zheff deserves to know his other mother. Let's make it happen."

"Are you serious?" Rikii asked.

"I'm serious."

"What about the recording? Tia isn't even going to hear you once she gets a whiff of that recording," Rikii stated.

"Baby, you and I are a force, and nothing—and I mean nothing—can stop us."

Rikii looked at Miles and smiled. "You're just saying nice things to get me back in that transport."

"Is it working? Because if it is, wait till you hear what I have to say to get you in my bed."

"Oh, is that right?"

Miles stood up and offered a hand to Rikii, who took it and stood up.

"Always stronger together," Miles said.

27

Way, Way, Way Back in the Day...

"What are you doing, boy?" Buddha Bane yelled at his son. Buddha's face was an emotional wreck that was decorated with muck and blood from the ongoing battle.

"Let me go, Father," Jax ordered as he struggled to wiggle his arm free from his father's great strength.

"There are plenty of women, Jax! None are worth losing your life for!" Buddha yelled.

He knew it was not the best advice, but what else could he say? A year ago, he believed his son to be dead, later to be told that he was taken captive and sold into slavery.

Jax escaped his father's grasp. "Well, this one is."

Jax cut down enemies with his sword until he came upon a riderless warhorse, and with haste, he mounted it. Jax ordered the warhorse to enter the fray of fighting men as he made his way to Astra. Jax could see her and his band of friends swinging their blades wildly, all doing their best to keep attackers at bay. Jax maneuvered majestically, cutting down those beneath him as he and the warhorse drove forward.

At least a hundred yards from her, Jax thought.

Jax rode hard, but the battle was so tight that the momentum of the warhorse alleviated, and that was a grave mishap. Warriors used their spears, swords, and other weapons to bring down the horse, and Jax became trapped under the beast and surrounded by warriors.

Fuck, fuck, fuck, Jax thought as tried to free himself from the warhorse.

He used his sword and flexibility to defend himself from men trying to stab him.

Blood gushed onto Jax as his attackers were dismembered violently.

"Come on, boy!" Buddha yelled as he lifted the horse just enough for Jax to free himself.

"Jax, please, I need to get you to safety!"

Jax ignored his father, something he never did. Jax rose with his sword and began cutting, stabbing, and swinging at anyone standing between him and Astra. Jax ignored the fatigue in his legs and his arms. He never looked back to even see if his father was behind him; he just kept fighting, fighting until he got to her.

"Astra!" Jax roared as he fought. He screamed her name, her name giving him the push he needed.

"Jax!" Astra screamed back.

Jax heard her scream his name, and he fought with everything he had to get to her. He cared not for his dying comrades under his feet; he cared not about the enemies whose souls he took. He fought like a barbarian, true to his Bane bloodline, losing all techniques that his instructors taught him; this was not the time to look pretty in battle.

"Jax, I'm here!" Astra screamed out.

Astra was covered in blood and mud, some of her cheap armor was missing, and her clothes were torn. Jax cleared a path, and he could see her. She was at the end of her stamina. Jax cut down the remaining enemies around her and took her in his arms.

"So you did keep your word," she said through heavy breaths.

Jax looked at her, her black face covered with tattoos of her tribe, her hair growing back from it being all cut off by the slave traders.

"I told you I would," Jax said. "Stay behind me. We need to get back to my father."

As the words escaped Jax's mouth, he realized that in his rage, he lost track of where his father was.

"Jax, I'm tired. I can't move my leg," Astra said.

"You have to, Astra. You got to push through. Don't worry, I'm right here with you," Jax responded.

"No, Jax," Astra said as she looked down at her leg, making Jax look down. There was an arrow lodged in Astra's thigh, and only her adrenaline was keeping her upright.

"See? I told you, dumbass. I can't move my leg," Astra said.

Jax threw Astra's arm over his neck and assisted her. He knew death was inevitable at this moment because there was no way he could swing a sword and assist Astra at the same time, but he was not going to leave her. They had only seconds before more attackers were upon them, and Jax made the decision to pretend that they were not going to be a problem.

"Stop, Jax. Just listen to me. I want—"

Astra's sentence was interrupted because an arrow landed in her neck.

"No!" Jax yelled.

Astra's dead weight was too much for Jax to hold up with his own fatigued body, and they both slumped to the ground.

"Astra, I got you. You're fine. Trust me, you're going to make it," Jax pleaded with her.

Astra coughed up blood and fought for her last words. "I will find you again."

Astra took the blood from her mouth, scribbled a foreign word on Jax's forearm, and then became lifeless.

The battle stopped, men paused midswing, and mercy was shown to those who were about to receive the final blow. For all men, all warriors' eyes laid upon Jax Bane, whose roar of pain was so great that it shook the ground. The eyes of his audience widened at the golden cracks that began to appear on Jax's body.

They watched him rise from the dead corpse that he let fall from his arms. No one could move. Their minds couldn't fathom if Jax was a threat because his features were benevolent. The cracks in his skin radiated a heat that turned bystanders into ash, and yet none were able to move.

Buddha saw his son, and despite the trance that everyone else was in, he did not hesitate to move. With his full armor activated, he ran to his son; he saw something happening to him and took no chance on believing it was something good. But the closer he got, more and more men began to turn to ash, but Buddha pressed on.

"Jax!" Buddha yelled, the fear transparent in his voice.

At twenty yards away, Buddha yelled again, "Jax!"

At ten yards away, he yelled once more, "Jax!"

The cracks on Jax's body were so deep they resembled lava running down a volcano. Jax turned to his father's voice and saw the Lord of War running full speed toward him. Jax reached out for his father to grab him.

At five yards away, Buddha reached out to grab his son's hand, but he was halted, frozen still. His mind was conscious, his eyes were aware, and he stretched hard to grab his son's hand, for he was only inches away from him. Buddha couldn't talk; the only thing he could do was look at his son with the golden cracks.

"I'm sorry," Jax said as he exploded, turning everything into ash.

———— • ————

"What the fuck?" Miles said aloud as he woke from his dream. He looked over at Rikii and was happy that he didn't wake her. Miles lay in the bed but remained puzzled on his dream that felt more like a cinema than anything. He decided not to ponder it too much and went back to sleep.

———— • ————

Roman stared out the window as he listened to Amelia answer phone calls. Most of her conversations were her pleading with investors to remain calm, and the other half were legal teams telling her that they couldn't find a way out. Roman laughed at himself.

"The fuck is so funny, Roman?" Amelia snapped at him.

"Nothing at all, Amelia," Roman lied.

"We wouldn't be in this mess if you killed Miles."

"We wouldn't be in this mess if your employees knew how to keep their mouths shut," Roman said, amused.

"We are fucked. This can set us back decades, and Our Father will not be happy."

"Are you telling me that you have no solution?"

"Roman, everyone is pulling out. We are being fucking investigated for war crimes by various nations. We are being sued by a myriad of companies and civilians. What fucking solution?"

"We have brothers and sisters all over the world. Trust me, we will not take the fall for all this."

"Be that as it may, we as FPE are done. We lost the lands in Rae. Omar Hassan won't do business with us. Our Father is going to kill us Roman."

"May I interject?" Styles said. He sat in a chair, taking in the scene.

"Please, by all fucking means," Amelia responded.

"I just heard you say Omar Hassan will not be doing business with you and that you lost the lands in Rae."

"I did," Amelia said.

"How exactly did you lose the Lands in Rae if we sold them to you?" Styles asked.

"The Kurtazian government believes that we were going to construct more data centers in Rae to spy on them. They will not grant us the permits to let us or anyone to build on those lands," Roman answered.

"And with Omar looking like he's about to be the new sovereign supreme, we have no connects," Amelia added.

"Well, Tia Graves is going to be the next general of the Districts in the next election, a feat she was only able to pull off when she managed to coerce Omar into a deal, a deal that I brokered," Styles said.

"I'm not seeing your point. Your cousin will not be convinced to enter into a new deal especially with this shit on the media," Roman said.

"You people, even in your metal bodies, still cannot see the bigger picture. If Tia is the general, then who is left to run the foundation? And if you say Bloody Hands, then I no longer have a need to work for you," Styles said as he stood up to take his leave.

Amelia smiled. "And you're going to help us get our permits to build on the land?"

"Tia won't be general for at least another two years, then another year for us to start breaking ground. Then on top of dealing with the exposer of FPE, we are looking at four to five years," Roman calculated.

"Don't see why there is a rush. You know, these types of matters take time," Styles said.

"And what of Bloody Hands?" Roman inquired.

"You don't have to worry about him. I sent him into an early retirement. I posted the wanted ad for his precious Rikii, so he won't risk coming back to the Districts, and if I sense he's anywhere near our plans, I will make Rikii a global fugitive," Styles said.

There was a moment of silence. Amelia and Roman looked at Styles, their minds trying to fathom if Styles was up to something, but they had no other option but to entertain his idea.

"Now that is interesting," Amelia said.

"We would have to run it by Our Father, but it can definitely work."

"Well, I will let you figure it out among yourselves. You know how to reach me," Styles said, taking his leave.

"I think we got this all wrong," Roman said.

"What you mean?" Amelia responded.

"I don't think it was Miles and Tia that we should have been worried about."

EPILOGUE

Miles walked out onto the flybridge of his fancy yacht with only a towel wrapped around his waist. He wore his hair natural, his kinky curls falling past his shoulders.

Miles breathed in the fresh air and enjoyed being detached from the problems of the world, the joys of being retired.

Rikii woke up and joined Miles. She was completely naked, her hair still a pixie cut, but she abandoned the finger waves. She stood next to Miles, grabbed his arm, and started kissing it. She made a point to put her slight morning erection on him.

"What are you thinking about?" Rikii asked.

"I'm trying to figure out why the sun keeps rising every morning. Does it not know that it would never shine as bright as you?" Miles responded, looking into Rikii's eyes.

Rikii removed Miles's towel and stood in front of him. She placed her hands around Miles's neck, and he bent down to kiss her, their tongues delighting in each other's touch. Rikii, feeling Miles grow erect from their kiss, squatted down, still on her toes, and took Miles into her mouth.

She started off slow, working her tongue around the head of his cock, before fully opening her throat for him. She looked up at Miles, who was engulfed in pleasure. Rikii made sure to get as much saliva on him as possible as she made the sounds of her enjoyment.

Miles grabbed Rikii by her hair and stood her up. He gripped her by the jaw, making sure her mouth remained opened; he spat in her mouth and kissed her hard. Miles got on one knee; he took Rikii's privates into his mouth. Miles felt her squirm and gave her a few minutes of pleasure as he massaged her crevices.

"Turn around," Miles ordered.

Rikii did what she was told and was rewarded with Miles's tongue inside her hole. Rikii squirmed as Miles licked her and stroked her cock simultaneously.

"Fuck, baby," Rikii moaned. "Goddamn, I'll kill for you," she whispered out. "Take it, Miles. You take what's yours!" Rikii shouted out.

Miles stood up. He spat into his hand and added more saliva to his privates and inserted himself into Rikii.

Rikii was holding on to some railing when Miles took her left arm and put it behind her back. He took his other hand and held Rikii by her throat, and he thrusted.

"You are fucking mine," Miles grunted into her ear.

Miles released Rikii's arm, and she immediately went to stroke herself.

"Slow, baby, slow," Miles whispered to her.

Rikii obeyed and slowly stroked herself, the absent look on her face confirming her pleasure.

Miles slowed down his thrust to match her stroke.

"I'm there, Miles. I'm there," Rikii whined out.

"Let it go, baby. You release it all for me," Miles whispered into Rikii's ear.

"Miles, I fucking love you," Rikii said as she climaxed.

Miles pulled out of her and stroked himself until he released.

Miles picked Rikii up and escorted her to their bed.

"What do you want to do today, my love?" Rikii asked.

Miles smiled and kissed Rikii with only one thought in his head.

Sandy beaches and fruity drinks.

Scan QR Code to listen.
What I Like
by
M.U.R.K Entertainment

ACKNOWLEDGMENTS

I thank God for grace and mercy.

For all comic illustrations, I thank Thodoris Laourdekis.

For all music I thank Geoff Exquisite and all artists of M.U.R.K. Entertainment.

I would like to thank Betty Pacheco for reading the rough draft of this novel and sitting down to talk it through with me.

I would like to thank Albert Morgan for reading the rough draft of this novel and giving me feedback.

I would like to thank Colleen Vander Heyden for reading the rough draft of this novel and providing feedback.

Special thanks to my fiancé, Delaney, for giving me the headspace to write this story.

Milton Keynes UK
Ingram Content Group UK Ltd.
UKHW021838110324
439294UK00007B/133